recent years.

He was awarded the OBE for services to Literature

PARTHIAN BOOKS

A Human Condition

Rhys Davies

PARTHIAN BOOKS

Parthian
The Old Surgery
Napier Street
Cardigan
SA43 1ED
www.parthianbooks.co.uk

First published in 2001.
Reprinted in 2002.
All rights reserved.
© The estate of Rhys Davies.
ISBN 1-902638-18-2.

Typeset by NW.

Printed and bound by Colourbooks, Dublin.

With support from the Parthian Collective.

Cover: *A Human Condition* by Matt Jon.

A CIP catalogue record for this book is available from
the British Library.

Published with the assistance of

THE RHYS DAVIES TRUST

The publishers acknowledge the financial support of the
Rhys Davies Trust in the publication of this book.

The Rhys Davies Trust is a charity which has as its aims
the fostering of Welsh writing in English.

The Collected Stories of Rhys Davies, are available in
three volumes from Gomer Press.

Stories

'The human crisis is always a crisis of understanding'
Raymond Williams

THE DILEMMA OF CATHERINE FUCHSIAS

Puffed up by his success as a ship-chandler in the port forty miles away, where he had gone from the village of Banog when the new town was rising to its heyday as the commercial capital of Wales, Lewis had retired to the old place heavy with gold and fat. With him was the bitter English wife he had married for her money, and he built the pink-washed villas overlooking Banog's pretty trout stream. And later he had set up a secret association with an unmarried woman of forty who was usually called Catherine Fuchsias, this affair—she received him most Sunday evenings after chapel in her outlying cottage—eluding public notice for two years. Until on one of those evenings, Lewis, who for some weeks had been complaining of a 'feeling of fullness', expired in her arms on the bed.

In every village there is a Jezebel or the makings of one, though sometimes these descend virtuous to their graves because of lack of opportunity or courage, fear of gossip or ostracism. Lewis the Chandler was Catherine Fuchsias' first real lover, so that for her to lose him like that not only dreadfully shocked her but, it will be agreed, placed her in a serious dilemma. She was not a born bad lot and, as a girl, she had been left in the lurch by a sweetheart who had gone prospecting to Australia and never fulfilled his promise to call her there. Thereafter she had kept house for her father, a farm worker, until he had followed her mother into the burial-ground surrounding Horeb chapel, which she cleaned for five shillings a week; in addition she had a job three days a week in the little wool factory a mile beyond Banog. It was in Horeb chapel during service that Lewis first studied her and admired her egg-brown face, thick haunches and air of abundant health. Her cottage stood concealed on a bushy slope outside the village, and she had a great liking for fuchsias, which grew wonderfully in the rich lap of the cottage.

When her paramour died on her bed she at first refused to believe it, so pertinacious and active was he and so unlike her idea of a man of sixty-four. Nevertheless, she ran howling downstairs. There she madly poked the fire, flung the night cloth over the canary's cage, ran into the kitchen and swilled a plate or two in a bowl, straightened a mat, and tidied her hair. In the mirror *there* was her face, Miss Catherine Bowen's face, looking no different, a solid unharmed fact with its brown speckles. The autumn dusk beginning to arrive at the window was quiet and natural as the chirp of the bird winging past the pane. For a moment she listened to the grandfather clock ticking away the silence. Then, with a bustling haste, she filled the kettle, lit the oil cooker, took an apple tart out of a zinc safe, looked at it, and put it back. She stood still again. And groaned.

She crept half-way up the stairs and called: 'Mr. Lewis . . . Mr. Lewis, here I am! Just put the kettle on. Time's going, boy. Come down straight away . . . Mr. Lewis!' She raised her voice. 'Lewis, stir yourself, boy. Come on now!' Only the clock replied. She sat on the stairs and groaned. 'Lewis,' she whispered, 'there's a trick you are playing on me! Don't you come here again, I am offended . . . Yes, offended I am. I'll go for a walk, that's what I'll do. And don't you be here when I'm back.' She tramped noisily down the stairs, unlocked the front door, and slammed it behind her.

Bats were flying round the cottage. The sunflowers were hanging their half-asleep heads, and the old deep well among the luxuriant chrysanthemum bushes at the bottom of the garden, on which her eye rested for a dazed but speculative minute, stood in secret blue shadow. But she hurried out of the garden by the side gate where a path led into a coppice of dwarf trees and bushes. 'I'll go and pick mushrooms in Banner's fields, that's what I'll do,' she assured herself. 'Gone he'll be by the time I'm back.' But she did not descend the slope to the farm's fields. She scrambled into a ring of bushes and hid herself there on a patch of damp grass. One eye remained open in palpitating awareness, the other was half closed, as if she was in profound thought.

A bad shock can work wonders with a person's sensibility. Buried talents can be whisked up into activity, a primitive cunning reign again in its shady empire of old instincts. Or such a shock can create—women especially being given to escape into this—a fantasy of bellicose truth, a performance of the imagination that has nothing to do with hypocrisy but is the terrified soul backing away from reality. Catherine sprang up and hurried back to her whitewashed cottage. Already in the long dusky vale and the distant village a few lights shone out. She shot into the cottage and ran upstairs.

'Well, Mr. Lewis,' she exclaimed loudly, 'better you are after your rest?' She went close to the bed and peered down at the stout dusky figure lying on the patchwork quilt. 'Well now, I am not liking the look of you at all,' she addressed it, half scoldingly. 'What have you taken your jacket off for? Hot you were? Dear me, quite bad you look. Best for me to fetch your wife and the doctor. But you mustn't lie there with your coat off or a cold you will catch.' Volubly tut-tutting, she lit a candle and set about the task. Already in the hour that had elapsed, he had begun to stiffen somewhat. She perspired and groaned, alternately blanching and going red. He was heavily cumbersome as a big sack of turnips: she was obliged to prop up his back with a small chair wedged against the bedsteads. Luckily he had removed only his jacket, but (since of late he had got stouter) this, which was of chapel-black vicuna, fitted tight as the skin of a bladder of lard. Downstairs, the grandfather clock ticked loud and hurried.

Finally, buttoned up complete, he rested tidy, and she staggered back sweating. To lay out her father she had got the assistance of the blacksmith's wife.

For a minute she stood in contemplation of her work, then ran downstairs to fetch up his hat, umbrella, and hymn-book. She dropped the umbrella beside the bed, placed the hat on the bedside table, and laid the hymn-book on the quilt as though it had fallen from his hand. And all the time she uttered clamorous remarks of distress at his condition—'Oh, Mr. Lewis, you didn't ought to have taken a walk unwell like you are. Climbing! Lucky I saw you leaning over my gate. Dropped dead in the road you might have, and stayed there all night and got bitten by the stoats! You rest quiet now, and I won't be long.' At another thought she placed a glass of water by the bedside. Then, giving her own person a quick look-over, she put on a raincoat and a flowered hat, blew out the candle, and hastened from the cottage. It was past nine o'clock and quite dark, and she never rode her bicycle in the dark.

Half an hour later she banged at the costly oaken door of the pink villa, calling excitedly: 'Mrs. Lewis, Mrs. Lewis, come to your husband!' Milly Jones, the servant, opened the door, and Catherine violently pushed her inside. 'Where's Mrs. Lewis? Let me see her, quick.' But Mrs. Lewis was already standing, stiff as a poker, in the hall.

'Catherine Fuchsias it is!' exclaimed Milly Jones, who was a native of Banog. 'Why, what's the matter with you?'

Catherine seemed to totter. 'Come to your husband, Mrs. Lewis, crying out for you he is! Oh dear,' she groaned, 'run all the way I have, fast as a hare.' She gulped, sat on a chair, and panted: 'Put your hat on quick, Mrs. Lewis, and tell Milly Jones to go to Dr. Watkins.'

Mrs. Lewis, who had the English reserve, never attended chapel, and also unlikably minded her own business, stared hard.

'My husband has met with an accident?' she asked, precise and cold.

'Wandering outside my gate I found him just now!' cried Catherine. 'Fetching water from my well I was, and saw him swaying about and staring at me white as cheese. "Oh, Mr. Lewis," I said, "what is the matter with you, ill you are? Not your way home from chapel is this!" . . . "Let me rest in your cottage for a minute," he said to me, "and give me a glass of water, my heart is jumping like a toad." . . . so I helped him in and he began to grunt awful, and I said: "Best to go and lie down on my poor father's bed, Mr. Lewis, and I will run at once and tell Mrs. Lewis to fetch Dr. Watkins." . . . Bring the doctor to him quick, Mrs. Lewis! Frightened me he has and no one to leave with him, me watering my chrysanthemums and just going to lock up for the night and seeing a man hanging sick over my gate—' She panted and dabbed her face.

Milly Jones was already holding a coat for her mistress, who frowned impatiently as Catherine went on babbling of the fright she had sustained. Never a talkative person, the Englishwoman only said, abrupt: 'Take me to your house . . . Milly, go for the doctor and tell him what you've just heard.' And she did not say very much as she stalked along beside Catherine, who still poured out a repeating wealth of words.

Arrived at the dark cottage, Catherine bawled comfortingly on the stairs: 'Come now, Mr. Lewis, here we are. Not long I've been, have I?'

'You ought to have left a light for him,' remarked Mrs.

Lewis on the landing.

'What if he had tumbled and set the bed on fire?' said Catherine indignantly. In the heavily silent room she struck a match and lit the candle. 'Oh!' she shrieked.

Mrs. Lewis stood staring through her glasses. And then, in a strangely fallen voice, said: 'John! . . . John!' Catherine covered her face with her hands, crying in dramatic woe. 'Hush, *woman...* hush,' said Mrs. Lewis sternly.

Catherine moved her hands from her face and glared. *Woman,* indeed! In her own house! When she had been so kind! But all she said was: 'Well, Mrs. Lewis, enough it is to upset anyone with a soft heart when a stranger dies in her house . . . *Why,*' she began insidiously, 'was he wandering in the lanes all by himself in his bad state? Poor man, why is it he didn't go home after chapel? Wandering lost outside my gate like a lonely orphan child!'

Mrs. Lewis, as though she were examining someone applying for a place in her villa kitchen, gave her a long, glimmering look. 'Here is the doctor,' she said.

'Yes indeed,' Catherine exclaimed, 'and I am hoping he can take Mr. Lewis away with him in his motor.' The glance she directed at the corpse was now charged with hostility. 'He is a visitor that has taken advantage of my poor little cottage.' And was there a hint of malice in her manner as she swung her hips past Mrs. Lewis, went to the landing, and called down the stairs: 'Come up, Dr. Watkins. But behind time you are.'

Having verified the death and listened to Catherine's profuse particulars of how she had found him at the gate and strained herself helping him up the stairs, Dr. Watkins, who was of local birth and a cheerful man, said: 'Well, well, only this evening it was I saw him singing full strength in chapel, his chest out like a robin's. Pity he never would be a patient of mine. "You mind that heart of yours, John Lewis," I told him once, free of charge, "and don't you smoke, drink, or sing." Angina he had, sure as a tree got knots.'

'He liked to sing at the top of his voice,' agreed Mrs. Lewis. She took up the hymn-book from the quilt, turned quickly to Catherine, and demanded: 'Did he take this with him to bed, ill as he was?'

'No!' Catherine's voice rang. With Dr. Watkins present, the familiar local boy, she looked even more powerful. 'After I had helped him there and he laid a minute and went a better colour, I said: "Now, Mr. Lewis, you read a hymn or two while I run off, strength they will give you".'

'But you put the candle out!' pounced Mrs. Lewis. 'It must have been getting quite dark by then.'

'There,' Catherine pointed a dramatic finger, 'is the box of matches, with the glass of water I gave him.' She stood aggressive, while Dr. Watkins's ears moved. 'Candles can be lit.'

'This,' proceeded Mrs. Lewis, her eyes gazing around and resting in turn on a petticoat hanging on a peg and the women's articles on the dressing table, '*this* was your father's room?'

'Yes,' Catherine said, defiant; 'where he died and laid till

14

they took him to Horeb. But when the warm weather comes, in here I move from the back; cooler it is and the view in summer same as on the postcards that the visitors buy, except for the old Trout Bridge . . . What are you so inquisitive about?' She began to bridle. 'Tidy it is here, and no dust. You would like to look under the bed? In the chest?'

Mrs. Lewis, cold of face, turned to the doctor. 'Could you say how long my husband has been dead?'

He made show of moving the corpse's eyelids, pinching a cheek, swinging an arm. 'A good two hours or more,' he said with downright assurance.

'Then,' said Mrs. Lewis, 'he must have been dead when he walked up those stairs! It takes only half an hour to reach my house from here.' She turned stern to Catherine: 'You said you came running to me as soon as you helped him up here to your father's room.'

'A law of the land there is!' Catherine's voice rang. 'Slander and malice is this, and jealous spite!' She took on renewed power and, like an actress towering and swelling into rage, looked twice her size. 'See,' she cried to Dr. Watkins, 'how it is that kind acts are rewarded, and nipped by a serpent is the hand of charity stretched out to lay the dying stranger on a bed! Better if I had let him fall dead outside my gate like a workhouse tramp and turned my back on him to water my Michaelmas daisies. Forty years I have lived in Banog, girl and woman, and not a stain small as a farthing on my character.' With her two hands she pushed up her inflated breasts as though they hurt her. 'Take him out of my

15

house,' she sang in crescendo, 'my poor dead visitor that can't rise up and tell the holy truth for me. No husband, father, or brother have I to fight for my name. Take him!'

'Not possible tonight,' said Dr. Watkins, bewildered but appreciative of Catherine's tirade. 'Late and a Sunday it is, and the undertaker many miles away.'

'The lady by there,' said Catherine, pointing a quivering finger, 'can hire the farm cart of Peter the Watercress, if he can't go in your motor.'

'I,' said Mrs. Lewis, 'have no intention of allowing my husband to remain in this house tonight.' The tone in which she pronounced 'this house' demolished the abode to an evil shambles.

'Oh, oh,' wailed Catherine, beginning again, and moving to the bedside. 'John Lewis!' she called to the corpse, 'John Lewis, rise up and tell the truth! Swim back across Jordan for a short minute and make dumb the bitter tongue that you married! Miss Catherine Bowen, that took you innocent into her little clean cottage, is calling to you, and—'

Dr. Watkins, who had twice taken up his bag and laid it down again, interfered decisively at last, for he had been called out by Milly Jones just as he was sitting down to some slices of cold duck. 'Hush now,' he said to both women, a man and stern, 'hush now. Show respect for the passed away . . . A cart and horse you would like hired?' he asked Mrs. Lewis. 'I will drive you to Llewellyn's farm and ask them to oblige you.'

'And oblige me too!' Catherine had the last word, swinging her hips out of the room.

The corpse, though not much liked owing to its bragging when alive, was of local origin, and Llewellyn the Farmer agreed readily enough to disturb his stallion, light candles in the cart lanterns, and collect two village men to help carry the heavy man down Catherine Fuchsias' stairs. Already the village itself had been willingly disturbed out of its Sabbath night quiet, for Milly Jones, after calling at the doctor's, was not going to deprive her own people of the high news that rich Mr. Lewis had mysteriously been taken ill in Catherine's cottage. So when the farm cart stopped to collect the two men, news of the death was half expected. Everybody was left agog and expectant of the new week being a full one. What had Mr. Lewis been doing wandering round Catherine's cottage up there after Chapel? Strange it was. Married men didn't go for walks and airings after chapel.

On Monday morning, before the dew was off her flowers, Catherine's acquaintance, Mrs. Morgans, who lived next door to the Post Office, bustled into the cottage. 'Catherine, dear,' she exclaimed, peering at her hard. 'What is this, a man dying on your bed!'

'My father's bed,' corrected Catherine. And at once her body began to swell. 'Oh, Jinny Morgans, my place in Heaven I have earned. I have strained myself,' she moaned, placing her hands round her lower middle, 'helping him up the stairs after I found him whining like an old dog outside my gate. A crick I have got in my side too. So stout he was, and crying to lay down on a bed. I thought he had eaten a toadstool for a mushroom in the dark.'

'What was he doing, walking about up here whatever?' Mrs. Morgans breathed.

'Once before I saw him going by when I was in my garden. He stopped to make compliments about my fuchsias— Oh,' she groaned, clasping her stomach, 'the strain is cutting me shocking.'

'Your fuchsias—' egged on Mrs. Morgans.

'Very big they hung this year. And he said to me, "When I was a boy I used to come round here to look for tadpoles in the ponds." Ah!' she groaned again.

'Tadpoles,' Mrs. Morgans nodded, still staring fixed and full on her friend, and sitting tense with every pore open. As is well known, women hearken to words but rely more on the secret information obtained by the sense that has no language.

Catherine, recognising that an ambassador had arrived, made a sudden dive into the middle of the matter, her hands flying away from her stomach and waving threatening. And again she went twice her size and beat her breast. 'That jealous Mrs. Lewis,' she shouted, 'came here and went smelling round the room nasty as a cat. This and that she hinted, with Dr. Watkins there for witness! A law of slander there is,' she shot a baleful glance at her visitor, 'and let one more word be said against my character and I will go off straight to Vaughan Solicitor and get a letter of warning sent.'

'Ha!' said Mrs. Morgans, suddenly relaxing her great intentness. 'Ha!' Her tone, like her nod, was obscure of meaning, and on the whole she seemed to be reserving judgment.

Indeed, what real proof was there of unhealthy proceedings having been transacted in Catherine's cottage? Mrs. Morgans went back to the village with her report and that day everybody sat on it in cautious meditation. In Catherine's advantage was the general dislike of proud Mrs. Lewis, but, on the other hand, a Jezebel, for the common good and protection of men, must not be allowed to flourish unpunished! All day in the Post Office, in the Glyndwr Arms that evening, and in every cottage and farmhouse, the matter was observed from several loquacious angles.

On Wednesday afternoon Mr. Maldwyn Davies, B.A., the minister of Horeb, climbed to the cottage, and was received by his member and chapel cleaner with a vigorous flurry of welcome. Needlessly dusting a chair, scurrying for a cushion, shouting to the canary, that at the minister's entrance began to chirp and swing his perch madly, to be quiet, Catherine fussily settled him before running to put the kettle on. In the kitchen she remembered her condition and returned slow and clasping herself. 'Ah,' she moaned, 'my pain has come back! Suffering chronic I've been off and on, since Sunday night. So heavy was poor Mr. Lewis to take up my stairs. But what was I to be doing with a member of Horeb whining outside my gate for a bed? Shut my door on him as if he was a scamp or a member of the Church of England?'

'Strange,' said Mr. Davies, his concertina neck, that could give forth such sweet music in the pulpit, closing down into his collar, 'strange that he climbed up here so far, feeling unwell.' He stared at the canary as if the bird held the explanation.

'Delirious and lighted up he was!' she cried. 'And no wonder. Did he want to go to his cold home after the sermon and singing in chapel? No! Two times and more I have seen him wandering round here looking full up with thoughts. One time he stopped at my gate and had praises for my dahlias, for I was watering them. "Oh, Mr. Lewis," I said to him, "what are you doing walking up here?" and he said, "I am thinking over the grand sermon Mr. Davies gave us just now, and I would climb big mountains if mountains there were!" Angry with myself I am now that I didn't ask him in for a cup of tea, so lonely was he looking. "Miss Bowen," he said to me, "when I was a boy I used to come rabbiting up here".'

'Your dahlias,' remarked Mr. Davies, still meditatively gazing at the canary, 'are prize ones, and the rabbits a pest.'

'Oh,' groaned Catherine, placing her hand round her lower middle, 'grumbling I am not, but there's a payment I am having for my kindness last Sunday!... Hush,' she bawled threateningly to the canary, 'hush, or no more seed today.'

Mr. Davies, oddly, seemed unable to say much. Perhaps he, too, was trying to sniff the truth out of the air. But he looked serious. The reputation of two of his flock was in jeopardy, two who had been nourished by his sermons, and it was unfortunate that one of them lay beyond examination.

'Your kettle is boiling over,' he reminded her, since in her exalted state she seemed unable to hear such things.

She darted with a shriek into the kitchen, and when she came back with a loaded tray, which she had no difficulty in carrying, she asked: 'When are you burying him?'

'Thursday, two o'clock. It is a public funeral... You will go to it?' he asked delicately.

This time she replied, sharp and rebuking: 'What, indeed, *me*? Me that's got to stay at home because of my strain and can only eat custards? Flat on my back in bed I ought to be this minute... Besides,' she said, beginning to bridle again, 'Mrs. Lewis, the *lady*, is a nasty!' She paused to take a long breath and to hand him a buttered muffin.

'Her people are not our people,' he conceded, and pursed his lips.

Fluffing herself up important, and not eating anything herself, Catherine declared: 'Soon as I am well I am off to Vaughan Solicitor, to have advice.' Black passion began to scald her voice; she pointed a trembling finger ceilingwards. 'Up there she stood in the room of my respected father, with Dr. Watkins for witness, and her own poor husband not gone cold and his eyes on us shiny as buttons, and her spiteful tongue made remarks. Hints and sarcastic! Nearly dropped dead I did myself... The hand stretched out in charity was bitten by a viper!' She began to swell still more. 'Forty years I have lived in Banog, clean as a whistle, and left an orphan to do battle alone. Swear I would before the King of England and all the judges of the world that Mr. John Lewis was unwell when he went on the bed up there! Sweat I would that my inside was strained by his weight! A heathen gypsy would have taken him into her caravan! Comfort I gave him in his last hour. The glass of water by the bed, and a stitch in my side racing to fetch his wife, that came here stringy and black-natured as a bunch of dry old seaweed and made evil remarks for thanks… Oh!' she clasped her breasts as if they would explode, 'if justice there is, all the true tongues of Banog must rise against her and drive the bad-speaking stranger away from us over the old bridge. Our honest village is to be made nasty as a sty, is it? No!'

Not for nothing had she sat all these years in close attention to Mr. Davies's famous sermons, which drew persons from remote farms even in winter. And, as she rocked on her thick haunches and her voice passed from the throbbing of harps to the roll of drums, Mr. Davies sat at last in admiration, the rare admiration that one artist gives to another. She spoke with such passion that, when she stopped, her below-the-waist pains came back and, rubbing her hands on the affected parts, she moaned in anguish, rolling up her big moist eyes.

'There now,' he said, a compassionate and relenting note in his voice, 'there now, take comfort.' And as he pronounced: 'There must be no scandal in Banog!' she knew her battle was won.

'Put your hands by here,' she cried, 'and you will feel the aches and cricks jumping from my strain.'

But Mr. Davies, a fastidious look hesitating for a moment across his face, accepted her word. He took a slice of apple tart and ate it, nodding in meditation. A woman fighting to preserve the virtue of what, it is said, is the most priceless treasure of her sex is a woman to be admired and respected. Especially if she is a Banog one. And it was natural that he was unwilling to accept that two of his members could have forgotten themselves so scandalously. Nevertheless, as Catherine coiled herself down from her exalted though aching state and at last sipped a little strong tea, he coughed and remarked: 'It is said that nearly every Sunday night for two years or more Mr. Lewis never arrived home from chapel till ten o'clock, and no trace is there of his occupation in these hours. "A walk," he used to tell in his home, "a Sunday-night walk I take to think over the sermon." That is what the servant Milly Jones has told in Banog, and also that in strong doubt was Mrs. Lewis concerning those walks in winter and summer.'

'Then a policeman she ought to have set spying behind him,' said Catherine, blowing on a fresh cup of tea with wonderful assurance. 'Oh, a shame it is that the dead man can't rise up and speak. Oh, wicked it is that a dead man not buried yet is turned into a goat.' Calm now, and the more impressive for it, she added: 'Proofs they must bring out, strict proofs. Let Milly Jones go babbling more, and *two* letters from Vaughan Solicitor I will have sent.'

'Come now,' said Mr. Davies hastily, 'come now, the name of Banog must not be bandied about outside and talked of in the market. Come now, the matter must be put away. Wind blows and wind goes.' He rose, gave a kind nod to the canary, and left her.

He would speak the decisive word to silence offensive tongues. But, as a protest, she still stayed retreated in the cottage; serve them right in the village that she withheld herself from the inquisitive eyes down there. On Friday morning the milkman told her that Mr. Lewis had had a tidy-sized funeral the previous day. She was relieved to hear he was safely in the earth, which was the home of forgetfulness and which, in due course, turned even the most disagreeable things sweet. After the milkman had gone she mixed herself a cake of festival richness, and so victorious did she feel that she decided to put an end to her haughty exile on Sunday evening and go to chapel as usual; dropping yet another egg in the bowl, she saw herself arriving at the last minute and marching to her pew in the front with head held high in rescued virtue.

On Saturday morning the postman, arriving late at her out-of-the-way cottage, threw a letter inside her door. A quarter of an hour later, agitated of face, she flew from the cottage on her bicycle. The village saw her speeding through without a look from her bent-over head. She shot past the Post Office, Horeb chapel, the inn, the row of cottages where the nobodies lived, past the house of Wmffre, the triple-crowned bard whose lays of local lore deserved to be better known, past the houses of Mr. Davies, B.A., and Mrs. Williams Flannel, who had spoken on the radio about flannel-weaving, past the cottage of Evans the Harpist and Chicago Jenkins, who had been in jail in that place, and, ringing her bell furious, spun in greased haste over the cross-roads where, in easier times, they hanged men for sheep stealing. She got out on to the main road without molestation.

'Judging,' remarked Mrs. Harpist Evans in the Post Office, 'by the way her legs were going on that bike the strain in her inside has repaired quite well.'

It was nine miles to the market town where Vaughan the

solicitor had his office, which on Saturday closed at midday. She stamped up the stairs, burst into an outer room, and demanded of a frightened youth that Mr. Vaughan attend to her at once. So distraught was she that the youth skedaddled behind a partition of frosted glass, came back, and took her into the privacy where Mr. Vaughan, who was thin as a wasp and had a black hat on his head, hissed: 'What are you wanting? Closing time it is.' Catherine, heaving and choking, threw down the letter on his desk and, after looking at it, he said, flat: 'Well, you can't have it yet. Not till after probate. You go back home and sit quiet for a few weeks.' Accustomed to the hysteria of legatees, and indeed of non-legatees, he turned his back on her and put a bunch of keys in his pocket.

She panted and perspired. And, pushing down her breasts, she drew out her voice, such as it was— 'Oh, Mr, Vaughan,' she whimpered, 'it is not the money I want. Come I have to ask you to let this little business be shut up close as a grave.' A poor misused woman in mortal distress, she wiped sweat and tears off her healthy country-red cheeks.

'What are you meaning?' He whisked about impatient, for at twelve-five, in the bar-parlour of the Blue Boar, he always met the manager of the bank for conference over people's private business.

She hung her head ashamed-looking as she moaned: 'A little favourite of Mr. Lewis I was, me always giving him flowers and vegetables and what-not free of charge. But bad tongues there are in Banog, and they will move quick if news of this money will go about.'

'Well,' he said, flat again, 'too late you are. There is Mrs. Lewis herself knowing about your legacy since Thursday evening, and—'

Catherine burst out: 'But *she* will keep quiet for sure! She won't be wanting it talked that her husband went and left me three hundred pounds, no indeed! For *I* can say things that poor Mr. Lewis told me, such a nasty she was! It is of Horeb chapel I am worrying—for you not to tell Mr. Davies our minister or anyone else that I have been left this money.' She peeped up at him humble.

'Well,' he said, even flatter than before and, as was only proper, not sympathetic, 'too late you are again. Same time that I wrote to you I sent a letter to Mr. Davies that the chapel is left money for a new organ and Miss Catherine Bowen the cleaner left a legacy too: the letter is with him this morning. In the codicil dealing with you, Mr. Lewis said it was a legacy because your cleaning wage was so small and you a good worker.'

The excuse would have served nice but for that unlucky death on her bed. She groaned aloud. And as she collapsed on the solicitor's hard chair she cried out in anguish, entreating aid of him in this disaster. Pay him well she would if he preserved her good name, pounds and pounds.

'A miracle,' he said, 'I cannot perform.'

Truth, when it is important, is not mocked for long, even in a solicitor's office. The legatee went down the stairs with the gait of one whipped sore. She cycled back to her cottage as though using one leg, and, to avoid the village, she took a circuitous way, pushing the cycle up stony paths. At the cottage, after sitting in a trance for a while, she walked whimpering to the well among the chrysanthemums, removed the cover, and sat on the edge in further trance. An hour passed, for her thoughts hung like lead. She went into the dark night of the soul. But she couldn't bring herself to urge her body into the round black hole which pierced the earth so deep.

Then, on the horizon of the dark night, shone a ray of bright light. For the first time since the postman's arrival the solid untrimmed fact struck her that three hundred pounds of good money was hers. She could go to Aberystwyth and set up in partnership with her friend Sally Thomas who, already working there as a cook, wanted to start lodgings for the college students. The legacy, surprising because Mr. Lewis had always been prudent of pocket—and she had approved of this respect for cash, believing, with him, that the best things in life are free—the legacy would take her into a new life. She rose from the well. And in the cottage, shaking herself finally out of her black dream, she decided that Mr. Lewis had left her the money as a smack to his wife the nasty one.

No one came to see her. She did not go to chapel on the Sunday. Three days later she received a letter from Mr. Davies, B.A., inviting her to call at his house. She knew what it meant. The minister had sat with his deacons in special conclave on her matter, and he was going to tell her that she was to be cast out from membership of Horeb. She wrote declining the invitation and said she was soon to leave Banog to live at the seaside in quiet; she wrote to Sally Thomas at the same time. But she had to go down to the Post Office for stamps.

She entered the shop with, at first, the mien of an heiress. Two women members of Horeb were inside, and Lizzie Postmistress was slicing bacon. Catherine stood waiting at the Post Office counter in the corner. No one greeted her or took notice, but one of the customers slipped out and in a few minutes returned with three more women. All of them turned their backs on Catherine. They talked brisk and loud, while Catherine waited drawn up. Lizzie Postmistress sang: 'Fancy Lewis the Chandler leaving money for a new organ for Horeb!'

'The deacons,' declared the wife of Peter the Watercress, 'ought to say "No" to it.'

'Yes, indeed,' nodded the cobbler's wife; 'every time it is played members will he reminded.'

'Well,' said single Jane the Dressmaker, who had a tapemeasure round her neck, 'not the fault of the organ will that be.'

They clustered before the bacon-cutting postmistress. On a tin of biscuits, listening complacent, sat a cat. The postmistress stopped slicing, waved her long knife, and cried: 'Never would I use such an organ—no, not even with gloves on; and *I* for one won't like singing hymns to it.'

'A full members' meeting about *all* the business there ought to be! Deacons are men. Men go walking to look at dahlias and fuchsias—'

'And,' dared the cobbler's wife, 'drop dead at sight of a prize dahlia.'

Catherine rapped on the counter and shouted: 'Stamps!'

The postmistress craned her head over the others and exclaimed: 'Why now, there's Catherine Fuchsias! . . . Your inside is better from the strain?' she enquired. The others turned and stared in unison.

'Stamps,' said Catherine, who under the united scrutiny suddenly took on a meek demeanour.

'Where for?' asked the postmistress, coming over to the Post Office corner, and snatching up the two letters Catherine had laid on the counter. 'Ho, one to Mr. Davies, B.A., and one to Aberystwyth!'

'I am going to live in Aberystwyth,' said Catherine grandly.

'Retiring you are on your means?' asked Jane the Dressmaker.

'Plenty of college professors and well-offs in Aberystwyth!' commented Peter's wife.

'Well,' frowned the postmistress, as if in doubt about her right to sell stamps to such a person, 'I don't know indeed . . . What you wasting a stamp on this one for,' she rasped out, 'with Mr. Davies living just up the road? Too much money you've got?'

'Ten shillings,' complained unmarried Jane the dressmaker, 'I get for making up a dress, working honest on it for three days or more. Never will *I* retire to Aberystwyth and sit on the front winking at the sea.'

'What you going there so quick for?' asked the cobbler's wife, her eyes travelling sharp from Catherine's face to below and resting there suspicious.

'Two stamps.' The postmistress flung them down grudgingly at last, and took up Catherine's coin as if she was picking up a rotten mouse by the tail. 'Wishing I am you'd buy your stamps somewhere else.'

Catherine, after licking and sticking them, seemed to regain strength as she walked to the door, remarking haughtily: 'There's wicked jealousy when a person is left money! Jealous you are not in my shoes, now *and* before.'

But, rightly, the postmistress had the last word: 'A cousin I have in Aberystwyth. Wife of a busy minister that is knowing everybody there. A letter *I* must write to Aberystwyth too.'

THE SISTERS

Benjamin was the lodger. The two sisters kept house for their father, a collier, and Benjamin, a collier also, had lived with them for two years. The sisters' mother was dead. And they coveted Benjamin, who was young, fond of drink and generous with his money.

Deborah was twenty-nine and Cassie twenty-two; and although Deborah was rather superb with her big body and dark vindictive eyes, she feared the younger charms of her sister. Cassie was thin and pale; she, too, had glowing eyes, but her voice was like a saw, though her manner was lazy and languorous.

Tonight again they had been quarrelling. Latterly it had seemed that Benjamin favoured Deborah, and Cassie had just pronounced some dark accusations. The men were out in their public-houses, and Deborah was putting the supper things on the table, while Cassie sat before the fire, brooding and with an appearance of indifference. But she was burning with jealous hatred.

'You keep your nasty remarks to yourself,' Deborah said, her voice mocking with triumph. 'There's nearly sick with jealousy you are!'

'Ho!' scoffed Cassie, 'think I want him—him, a bellyful of

drink, as he always is? Disgusting and piggish are his ways. A sot he is, as Mrs. Evans, number 45, said.'

Deborah banged the china on the table and, her hands on her hips, her face thrust forward menacingly, she turned to her sister.

'You can call him names behind his back,' she cried, 'but think I don't know how you try to wheedle him when you get the chance? There's cunning you are when there's nobody but you and him in the house! I know. But cold as a rock he is with you. Ach y fi, know I do how you flaunt yourself before him like someone bad.'

Cassie looked at her, her narrowed eyes like ink. She jeered calmly: 'You shut up. When Benjamin has married you, then you can keep him. But you catch him first. But be quick, dear Deborah, because old and fat you are getting. And ugly, too.'

'Ho, ho,' shrieked Deborah, 'there's jealousy. It's settled between us, you old ape.'

'Liar.'

'Think a collier wants a lazy slut like you for a wife?' Deborah added. 'Said he has to me, a pigsty would Cassie make any home.'

'A pity you are so plain,' Cassie said. 'Married a long time ago you would have been if it wasn't for your looks. And not short-sighted is Benjamin, I know.'

Presently their father came in from the public-house. He was enormous, with a huge red nose and tiny red eyes. Beer seemed to ooze from his flesh, and when he spoke he snorted his

He held her tightly, but Deborah would not give in. At last she drew herself away and fastened her blouse. Her face was flushed as though with wine, and her eyes had a red tinge. Benjamin looked at her cringingly.

'Cruel you are,' he repeated.

'Go on!' she cried, 'respectable I am, not an old bitch of the gutters.'

She went up to bed. There were three bedrooms. Cassie occupied the back room, Deborah the middle, and the two men the front. Deborah locked her door. She heard Benjamin come up and mutter to himself as he undressed. Soon his snores were competing with those of her father. The last to sleep was Cassie, who had been brooding over a scheme that had come into her mind.

The next day the sisters were quarrelling again. Scarcely a day passed now without altercation over the lodger. And Deborah feared to leave the house when Benjamin might happen to come in. There was no trusting Cassie.

But Cassie waited her opportunity.

On Saturday nights the lodger came home later and more intoxicated than other nights. It was sometimes early morning when he came in to the sleeping house. And one Saturday night Cassie lay wide awake in her bed, waiting for the sound of the returning drunkard. Long past midnight she heard the latch of the front door click and was instantly out of bed.

Silently she passed down the stairs and followed the lodger into the dark living-room. While he was fumbling with matches she touched him with her hand and took the box away. The room was quite dark. Cassie did not utter a word.

Benjamin started, feeling her pressing body against him. Cassie put her mouth to his, that was like a piece of cold wet meat. And Benjamin's arms went round her with delight. He muttered:

'Ho, ho, Deborah darling! Changed your mind, have you? There's nice you are in your nightshirt!'

Later Cassie crept back to bed, leaving him there on the floor, where he spent most of the night. And she was up early the next morning, before anyone else. She smiled secretly to herself and also when Deborah came into the living-room, sullen and sinister as always. When the father came down they had breakfast together.

Cassie remarked: 'Very late was Benjamin last night.'

'Didn't hear him come in,' said her father.

'Nor I,' said Deborah shortly. 'There's lazy he is! Why doesn't he get up? A nuisance it is to keep breakfast waiting.'

'Leave the boy alone,' said the father. 'Sunday it is, so no matter.'

After breakfast Deborah began to wash the dishes, and Cassie, swinging a pail and singing softly, ran upstairs. She went into the front room. Benjamin lay in bed sleeping, his mouth wide open, his face blotched and hairy. Cassie shook him. His lids came unstuck slowly from his eyes, that were like gum.

'What d'you want?' he demanded irritably when he saw her.

'Wake up,' she whispered. 'Talk to you I want to.'

He looked at her as a bull looks, then closed his eyes.

She said sharply: 'No wonder you want to sleep, after your filth last night, you old pig. Wake up and say what you are going to do about it.'

His eyes opened quickly, and he looked at her with fear. He quavered: 'What a loose tongue has Deborah got! Fancy telling you! But her fault it was—she came downstairs after my body.'

'Deborah!' she cried harshly, 'it wasn't Deborah at all. Me it was. There's an old ruffian you are—taking advantage of me when I was on the way to the W.C.'

He stared at her foolishly, then grinned.

'There's no joke about it,' Cassie continued wrathfully. 'Go on, you dirty thing, to take advantage of me like that! Trouble I will make about it.'

'Keep you silent about this business, Cassie fach,' Benjamin entreated, his voice shaking with fear. 'Be a good and quiet girl and I will buy you a nice little present. Say what you want.'

'A gold wedding ring I want. You be honourable by me,' Cassie answered, showing her teeth.

Benjamin scratched his head, and Cassie sat on the bed and began to caress him coaxingly.

'Benjie bach,' she murmured, 'there's a good wife I will make! And a good time I will give you. Passionate I am.'

'Ach,' he cried, 'your old sister is after me too!'

'Ugly and an old witch is Deborah,' Cassie said. 'And suffer she will with her inside later on, the doctor says. A burden she would be on you.'

Before she went from the bedroom Cassie had extracted a promise of marriage from the lodger. She went downstairs in splendour and triumph. Deborah was alone in the kitchen.

'Benjamin has said that I am to be his wife,' Cassie announced in a mincing manner. 'Secret arrangements had we made, but I must tell you now, Deborah dear.'

Deborah turned round quickly. Her face was the colour of heavy dough. The water from the dish-cloth in her hands dripped on the floor.

'Liar! she exclaimed.

Cassie put her nose high in the air,

'Just settled it we have,' she said carelessly.

Fear and suspicion struggled on Deborah's face. Then she flung the dishcloth at her sister's elevated profile. Cassie shrieked.

'You sly snake,' Deborah screamed, 'sly and cunning!'

The father came in from the back-yard and found his daughters struggling together. He went back to his pigeons. After some damage to each other the sisters separated, and Cassie ran to fetch Benjamin. She brought him down in his trousers and shirt.

'You tell her,' she cried, pointing to the weeping Deborah in the corner, 'tell her it's me you are marrying.'

'Is it true, Benjamin?' wept Deborah from her loosened hair.

Benjamin gazed at her like a sheep.

'It can't be helped,' he muttered, turning away. 'Where's my breakfast?'

Then Deborah rose in high wrath and scorn.

'Well, get married, you goats,' she cried derisively. 'There's a fine bag of flesh you are going to marry, Benjamin Jenkins! A lazy slut who won't wash her neck! Her old combs she wears for two months, being too lazy to wash them. Ah, the sly cat! Dirty outside and inside. My mother always said, what a blind frog will be the man who marries Cassie!'

'Natural it is to say evil lies when one is jealous,' said Cassie calmly. And she obsequiously attended to Benjamin's breakfast.

A perilous silence brooded in the house during the next few days. Deborah maintained an attitude of scornful disgust, but her haggard eyes gazed at her sister with a murderous hatred. In the nights she cried herself to sleep.

Then, after he had had his dinner and bath the following Saturday the lodger, instead of going to the public house, went to the railway station and took a ticket to one of the colliery towns in the Midlands of England. And it was Cassie who wept, a little later.

THE SONG OF SONGS

After Jane Hopkins had put her old rheumatic father to bed she went back to the living-room and stealthily and noiselessly laid supper for one—cold meat, a large bottle of stout, cheese and cake. Then she glanced at the clock and sat down.

She and her father lived alone. Old Hopkins was a retired publican and an irritable man bad-tempered with drink and rheumatism. Jane kept house for him and was thirty. She was a handsome woman—tall, graceful and with the lithe and untrammelled movements of a proud flame. Her face was flushed darkly, as though with sombre blood, and under their unquiet brows her eyes were heavy and glistened with a kind of sensual hostility. She was voluptuous and big; it was a mystery why she had never married. And she had few friends. Day after day for the last ten years she had lived alone with her father. Since her mother toppled drunkenly down the stairs of their public-house and broke her neck.

Until this winter. A friend had persuaded her to emerge from her aloof hostility and attend the weekly dances held in the Valley town-hall. And Jane had enjoyed these dances. She danced with ease and rhythm, giving herself wholly to the music and thinking nothing of the man who eagerly danced with her. For though she had a sombre and inimical face, the older of the young men liked her, as well as her graceful dancing. She had that indifference and contempt of them that roused their interest most. They liked to look into her eyes, that gazed back at them from their glistening darkness as from cells of disillusioned thought. And, watching her, her tall swaying body seemed full of a secretly burning passion. Many of them had asked to accompany her home...

Jane refused all except one, Evan Lewis. He had walked home with her for some weeks now. But when they got to her doorway and he attempted to put his arms round her she would push him away, with a strange laugh of contempt and desire, her mouth twisted rather uglily. But she liked him, she liked the sight of him. Only she could not rid herself of her old hatred, though her being expanded for his embrace...

They had quarrelled last week. He had attempted too much.

For an hour Jane sat before the dead fire, gazing, hardly without movement, into the ashes, her arms folded. When the clock struck the half-hour after midnight, she rose and for a few minutes stood gazing out of the window, a brutal grimace on her lips, though there seemed to be fear in her staring eyes. Then she went into the kitchen and let herself out of the house, walking softly over the grass of the back garden into the lane.

The night was still and brooding. The black hills rose up vastly and the sky was like dark blue stone, pricked with stars of frozen fire. In the far distance, at the end of the Valley, shone the smoky gold of the colliery lights. Noiselessly Jane crept on, drifting like a shadow down the lane, and emerged into the deserted main street.

On top of the hill that dips to the river and the mines she stopped and hid herself in a shop doorway. It was cold, and she shivered, listening to a shop sign that swung on its rusty hinges in the wind. A gas lamp shed a dull yellow light, and the chapel opposite and the squat black buildings about seemed like houses of the dead, silent and desolate.

But Jane's limbs stretched taut and expectant as she waited. Her heart beat thickly and the brutal grimace still twisted her lips. Now and again she peered round the doorway of the shop and down over the hill.

And presently someone appeared in the distance, slowly looming up. Jane listened, as the figure drew nearer, to the sound of heavy nailed boots striking the pavement. And that sound seemed to strike exultingly into her soul. Her eyes became hard and brilliant as the stars.

When the footsteps drew near the doorway she stepped out. Her throat beat nervously. But she drew her brows together and called out:

'Evan.'

The man stopped and peered at her.

'Jane Hopkins!' he exclaimed.

She looked at him with suffering eyes and was silent.

'Why, why . . .' he stammered, 'what's wrong?'

She stared at him for a while, then dropped her lids.

'Do you want to come back with me?' she asked painfully. He was silent, gazing at her bent head, astonished.

'I'm sorry I spoke nastily to you last week,' she continued. Still he was silent.

'Will you come with me?' she said at last, lifting her head with a sudden proud movement. But her face worked in agony.

'It's so late,' he answered in doubt, gazing at her almost in fear.

'Father is asleep long ago,' she said, taking one of his hands and caressing the fingers slowly. 'A nice supper I've laid for you, too. Then she dropped his hand angrily. 'Don't come if you're afraid,' she continued passionately. 'I thought last week—'

'Yes, yes, I want to come,' he said quickly.

She smiled.

'Take your boots off,' she said; 'make a noise they will.'

And in his socks he crept back to the house with her.

In the light of the living-room Jane looked at his smiling face and she too smiled a little, darkly. He was an engineer in the colliery and his face was smudged with black patches, his clothes filthy and smelling of oils and machinery. He was tall and powerful, like her, and an athlete, handsome. As he bent over the meat and stout she gazed at the back of his thick vigorous head.

She helped him to bread and drink.

'Like coming home to a wife this is,' he mumbled, his mouth full, the strong jaws moving like an animal's.

But later, when she had had her desire and felt his mouth

upon hers, a cold hate possessed her body, and she gazed with eyes of terror into his, that were drunken and obscene. She felt his mouth cling leech-like to her own, and her whole being wept silently with suffering. And she despised herself too.

When he had left, she looked, sickened, at the greasy plate he had eaten from, the tumbler with its ring of brown froth, the piece of bread blackened from his dirty hands. She could not touch them.

She went up to bed like a woman condemned and weaponless.

Sullenly she got up the next morning, returning hatred in her heart. She helped her father to dress, as usual, despising the task, the intimacy. He was a twisted, sordid mass of diseased flesh.

'There's impatient you are this morning,' the old man remarked irritably. 'Digging your old nails into me.'

'Be thankful someone you've got to do this for you at all,' Jane barked, fastening his collar with shaking fingers.

'What's the matter with you, gal!' he shouted wrathfully. 'Don't I keep you to do things for me?'

'Say the word and go I will. I can get married next week if I like.'

Her face was mottled with rage. She would have had the whole male sex blasted. And when she went downstairs and saw the supper things on the table her heart revolted in venom against the man she had admitted into her home the night before.

Yet, later in the day, she smiled secretly to herself.

Then the next day came a letter from Evan, full of love

and endearments. Jane laughed sardonically and put it in the fire. He asked her to meet him that evening, as he was finishing work early, and go for a walk on the mountains. She did not go.

Neither did she go to the dance that week. A few days later she had another letter from Evan. He wrote that he would come that night, the same time as before, from work. By then her fury had burned away and she waited his arrival with a jeering pity, knowing her power.

She saw his face at the window and gazed at it coldly, though with an inward fear. The face grinned lecherously. She went to the back door and said sharply:

'Don't stand there skulking like a dirty tom-cat.'

He stepped in with brisk familiarity and took hold of her arm.

'There now, Jane. I couldn't keep away for long. Say that glad you are to see me.'

'Waited you should have until I invited you,' she said resentfully.

But her resentment wore away and realising his supremacy she submitted at last. He laughed with delight.

'Dear little Jane,' he muttered childishly, 'there's love you I do.'

II

Early in the evening of the following Saturday there was a knock at the front door.

'Someone at the door, Jane,' called Hopkins nervously.

'I know,' Jane replied calmly, knowing who was there. 'Wait they must until I've finished wiping these dishes.'

After the knock had been repeated three times she went to the door. Evan stood on the step and smiled at her brilliantly. His face was polished and he wore a new navy blue suit and bowler hat. Jane looked down at his shining brown boots contemptuously.

'Told you I did you needn't come,' she said.

'I had to. Ask me in and don't be rude, Jane fach,' he answered, using the Welsh word of endearment lovingly. And he stepped in. She shrugged her shoulders, and they went into the front room, the stuffy never-used parlour. Evan put himself comfortably into a chair.

Jane leaned against the piano and looked at him with sullen indifference. The flesh seemed to hang wearily under her eyes, which were of that murky thickness that denotes a peevish liver. Her lips were protruding and brutal.

'Told you I did it was no use you coming any more,' she repeated.

He laughed. 'Coy!' he said, shaking his finger at her. 'Wants to be coaxed, does she?'

Her breasts lifted slowly, her nostrils expanded. His manner of possessive intimacy made her blood run rapid. She looked with hatred at the clean vigour of his face, the sprawling strength of his body.

'Don't tease,' he continued. 'Hurry up and come out for a walk. Something I've got to ask you.'

'I'm not going out with you,' she muttered.

He went over to her, pressed his large hands beneath her arms, extending the thumbs into those proud breasts.

'Leave me alone,' she moaned. 'Go away. I hate you.'

'Jane, Jane fach, don't be funny now. Come to ask you to marry me I have.'

'You silly old goat,' she shouted angrily, 'daft and blind you are. Let go of me.'

At last he was struck. He released her quickly.

'Oh!' he exclaimed, 'changed you have very soon.'

'Why think you that I want to marry you?' Jane spat out stridently, her eyes flaming derision.

'Led me to understand that you have . . .' he began hotly.

Jane lifted her head quickly and dangerously, like a cobra, and inclined it towards the door.

'Go,' she said histrionically.

He wanted her very much. He was suddenly entreating.

'Jane, love you I do. Listen to me now. And be wise. There's trouble you might have let yourself in for—'

At which she laughed, a hard sterile laughter, showing her teeth, and left him alone.

He found his way out and slammed the front door furiously.

Jane returned to the living-room and began humming to herself calmly.

'Who was it?' her father asked.

'Someone to see me.'

'Who was it?' her father repeated ominously.

'Why?' Her voice was profoundly hostile.

'Why!' he screamed. 'A right to know I've got, in my own house! Not a lodger am I, you sulky toad.'

'It was a man asking me to marry him,' she said with her insolent calmness.

'What!' he exclaimed. 'Good God!'

Jane continued to hum, knowing how it angered him.

'I hope to Christ you took him,' he snorted.

'No, I haven't,' she replied brightly, grinning down into his irate face. 'Not him,' she added.

And later that evening she put on her hat and coat and jauntily went out. She walked down to the little shop of J. J. Beynon, who does a brisk trade in cakes and sweets, at the base of the hill in the Square, where the tramcars stop and one can see life. Beynon was behind his counter and he looked joyfully at Jane over his wire spectacles as she entered the bright little shop.

'Go you through,' he said.

She went into his little living-room at the back, and Beynon followed her in. He was a frail little man, bald and hollow-looking. His eyes were dim and watery, and he trembled as though suffering from some ailment. But he was reputed to be rich, and, above all, possessed a shop, thus being respected throughout the Valley.

'Well now, Jane Hopkins,' he said, fondling her hands lovingly, 'this is a pleasure. Have you taken thought on the matter we spoke about last week?'

Jane put her strong arms about him and drew him up to

her lips as though he were a child.

'Yes, yes, get married we will very soon,' she answered.

And later she went into the shop, stood behind the counter, and said dreamily 'There's happy I'll be here, serving cakes and sweets! A little shop like this I've always wanted to have.'

THE DARLING OF HER HEART

The key of the cottage lay hidden in its customary place under the lavender clump beside the front porch. She unlocked the door and found everything as usual in the dusky living-room, its odour of Saturday morning wax-polishing still mingled with the scent of bunched herbs maturing under the pitted ceiling beams. The burnished brass candlesticks and the cherished pieces of old china on dresser and in cabinet were undisturbed; not a petal had fallen from the bowl of damask roses on the tawnily gleaming table. Nevertheless, all the house was desecrated.

As if following the intuition of her roused nose, its bird's curve quiveringly alert, Siân Prosser darted up the staircase of ancient oak rising direct from the living-room. She went into one of the two spick-and-span front rooms. A taut, small-assembled woman of sixty, in whose autumnal brown face the eyes had become blazingly renewed, she stood by the single-size bed for two or three minutes, while the sunset light thickened to a violet hue at the window. She stood as though gone into a trance in which unimpeachable knowledge was being given her.

Suddenly, and with furious speed, she stripped the bed,

taking the two blankets, the sheets, the pillow and bolster out to the landing and hurling them down the stairs. Next she dragged the mattress down the stairs and into the back garden. Getting the mattress through the gate into the rough, lumpy field behind the cottage was quite a task. After placing it over a molehill, so that air could circulate beneath it, she sped to fetch the pillow, bolster, sheets and blankets. Made locally, the blankets were of excellent Welsh flannel, which lasts for generations. She piled all on the humped mattress. Finally, she ran for a can of paraffin oil from the kitchen, liberally sprayed the big heap, and struck a match.

Flames spread over the heap with a soft, eating pleasure. Siân did not wait; the evening dew on the grass would prevent the flames spreading over the field. Back in the cottage, she peered up at the clock. Over an hour remained before the Rising Sun would close its doors. Everybody's social—and indeed private—habits are known in small country villages. Catrin Lloyd would be alone in her cottage until about half-past-ten. Siân hastened out, replacing the key under the lavender bush.

Hatless, walking with the trot of a vigorously small woman out on an important errand, she climbed a road bordered with fields in which, here and there, a farm cottage nestled. The Rising Sun, which she passed, lay cosily sunk in a fruiting apple orchard. Her own husband and the husband of the woman she was about to visit were inside it drinking together with the other village men in Saturday night freedom from woes. Not once had her husband picked a quarrel with Catrin's husband. But men were weak in such matters.

Arrived on the hill's crown, where, had she not been so heated, dowdy St. Teilo's church might have reminded her of Christian forbearance, Siân paused a moment. She looked back and, like Lot's wife, saw a glowing red confusion in the field behind her cottage. She resumed her trot with a pinched smile. A few lights began to gleam in windows of the cottages scattered spaciously in the well-ordered domain down the other side of the hill. Nobody else trod the road. At the bottom of the hill she turned off into a lane smelling of meadowsweet and clover, and at last came to a thatched, bulgy-walled old cottage.

Above its front flower garden, the twilit cottage stood pretty as a calendar picture, though in daylight it showed decayed and tumble-down, the thatch unkempt as the hair of the slut dwelling within. As her feet skipped up the garden path Siân could see, beyond an uncurtained window, an oil lamp burning inside. The windowsill was crowded with sickly potted plants, and, for some reason, Siân gave a grimace at sight of these: she had already peered contemptuously at the waiflike plants and bushes in the garden.

She gave the door a peremptory blow with her fist, lifted the latch without delay, and entered. It was her first visit to this cottage of Catrin's married life, and, intent on her errand though she was, her glance swept disdainfully over the gimcrack contents of the living-room. The front door opened into it immediately.

'Catrin Morgan,' commanded the visitor, using the maiden surname with a grimly pointed return to the past, 'get your feet out of that water and stand up.'

Catrin, who was giving her feet their Saturday soaking in a bowl on the hearthrug, astonishingly obeyed this hectoring order. At sight of Siân, the jaw of her big, round, nefarious face had dropped. Her milky eyes sidled as she dried her feet in a ragged towel and reached, bulkily, for her slippers. During this, a stream of calmly enunciated opinion came from Siân. She compared her erstwhile friend, not to the beasts of the fields, which country people respect, but to villainesses of Biblical and local fame, and she used adjectives applicable to evil human failings.

Catrin seemed unaffected by these preliminaries. 'Marching in!' she mumbled. An imposing but pulpy woman standing five or six inches taller than her opponent, she rose, and added: 'What do you want, Siân *Williams*?' Her own retaliatory use of Siân's maiden surname blew away not only forty years of married life, but a silence of the same period.

'You know why I've come.'

A large oval table stood between them. On it rested the oil lamp, its glass funnel unwashed for many a week. Catrin, her pale eyes absorbing without expression the menace shooting from those of the structurally-inferior woman opposite her, groped for her dentures on the mantelpiece and slipped them in. Possession of them seemed to give her a little more confidence, for she protested, with a certain amount of indignation: 'There's a knocker on my door. Marching in!' Perhaps it was shock that curtailed her and made her seem halted in stupor.

Siân, taking a short step round the table, came to the matter in hand. 'You set her on him! A stoat on a young rabbit!

Your red-haired daughter on *my* son!' She gave a quick yelp, such as a terrier might release. 'Plotting it all in revenge on me! No doubt you're hoping he gets her into trouble, so that he's got to marry her. *My* Oliver! *Your* Muriel! Ha!'

She took another step, and another, round the table, while Catrin, in obedient rhythm, backed round it. During Siân's next pronouncements they moved thus, in the manner of some solemn folkdance figure, twice round the table.

'You plotted with your Muriel to do her business even in my house! To spite me!... I saw them coming out when I came back early from my married daughter – *you* know I go to see her every Saturday evening, while my husband is in the Rising Sun and Oliver supposed to be gone on his bike to the cinema in Morpeth, the house locked up and the key under the lavender bush—*you* knew it all, and set your red-haired daughter to Delilah tricks with my son. *You* know he's my favourite, the darling of my heart—'

There was no hauteur, insult or mockery in her manner, only a bristling condemnation born of long breeding and decent taste. But still Catrin's faculties seemed to be entirely occupied in obediently, if warily, backing a step in unison with Siân's approach round the table, and still no word of denial or retaliation had come from her. All she said, repetitiously, was: 'Marching in!'

'For a month I've been smelling that something like this was going on. So I came back early tonight from my married daughter's house, an hour before my usual time. I saw them coming out when I was up on the main road. They went down into Bruchan Lane. Courting, are they?' Siân's beak darted towards the culprit she stalked, a degree faster, round the table. 'A red hair on the pillow!...I burned the bed in the field—' she allowed herself a menacing hiss as her hand moved towards the lamp— 'as I'll burn down this sty of a house, with you in it punched to Jerico, if that daughter of yours gives another look at my boy! See?'

Without further ado, she made a leap, head down, towards the momentarily paused woman. Accurate as a goat, she butted her head under Catrin's chin. There was a clicking sound of dentures sharply meeting. Otherwise, a choked gasp was all that Catrin manifested. But she backed a foolish step, thus allowing Siân space to take another leap and repeat the butt. Grunting and backing, Catrin flung out her arms. The main features of her face, blurred in fat, expressed an alarmed demise of the shifty elements governing her character. The physical pain of assault is trivial compared with revelatory power of its criticism, and blows (the only method, unfortunately, in some cases) are also a short cut to clarification of a disputatious matter. Catrin's girlhood friend had gone into action once more, and she knew what she was about.

'Now you can put your feet back in that water,' she pronounced, still amazingly brisk of wind.

Catrin, an expiring heap of plump mounds and flabbergasted limbs, collapsed into the fireside armchair. It was guilt again. Also, after forty years of silence, the incident was a tremendous recognition of undying bondage. Siân trotted to the door, looked back over her shoulder with a single threatening glance, and whisked out like a fox with dismissing celerity in its tail.

In the garden she heard a bellow. It came from delayed shock: all of Catrin's faculties moved cumbersomely. In the lane, additional bellows could be heard, swelling and lowing. Yet they were not truly agonised. Did they contain, besides hints of recovery, an undercurrent of satisfaction?

She got home with time to spare. A quarter of an hour later, Oliver walked in. His father would be there in a few minutes. It was their customary Saturday night arrival, in circumstances and time, for supper and bed.

Siân gave her son a fair preliminary hint. 'You didn't go to the cinema in Morpeth?' she said absently, without blunt questioning. 'When I came back from Barbara's I saw your bike in the shed.'

He sat down and took off his shoes, which had been beautifully polished by her and were now dust-spattered. 'I went for a walk with Ivor to the farm,' he said, 'to see his new sheepdog.'

Glad of the lie, which showed a proper sense of uneasiness, she said nothing and went on preparing the supper table. Oliver pulled on the soft calfskin slippers which had been a present from his mother on his nineteenth birthday a month ago. None of her other children had obtained such tributes as he enjoyed. She eyed him once or twice as she laid down crockery. He lit a cigarette without looking at her, but he went so far as to mention the price of the new sheepdog. She only said, 'Ah!' As she passed him, a frail breeze of opposition must have reached him.

'Ivor asked me to help in the trials,' he mumbled, still on the dog. She smiled at the back of his auburn head.

He was her best and different one, the last flower of her season. Particularly she delighted in his pale, well-bred little ears; her four other children, now out in the world, owned big purplish ones like their father. Oliver, by her determined efforts, had been put out to superior employment as a clerk in the Morpeth Rural Council offices; barring setbacks, he would never follow the agricultural pursuits of his family. But did his melancholy fine-cut nostrils still quiver at the aroma of ploughed soil? That he had responded to the wiles of Catrin's daughter, whose rufus hair was of a kind common in several unredeemed families of the district, deepened her suspicion that his physical delicacy was only a brittle shell.

When Prosser stumbled in, pompously holding his ham-shaped head erect, as always in liquor, she fetched the minced-liver faggots from the kitchen oven. At the same time she reiterated the scolding of hundreds of Saturday nights. He accepted it as his due, only interjecting a doomed 'Aye' and 'True, true!' and 'Correct as a tombstone, Siân,' his florid face smokily matured. His son sat waiting, slim legs stretched out, contrastingly not yet crystallised in his being.

'Well, come to the table, both of you,' Siân said.

She sat there in the quiet yellow lamplight. Her well-kept dishes shone, the hearth was shinily black as an empress housewife could make it; the herbs festooned on the beams sent down a pleasing odour to the delicious faggots which contained, together with apple and onion, a sprinkling of them. Even the clock, under its porcelain garland of cherub-borne flowers, seemed to tick in clear approval of its habitation.

At the table, Prosser's insecure attention became focused. At the side of his plate, instead of the usual everyday cup and saucer, stood a painted china mug. It had been taken from the glass cabinet of never-used domestic treasures. He gazed at the ceremonious piece in thunderstruck silence while Siân, talking of her routine visit to their daughter, dished out the Saturday night faggots. Did she, at the end of the meal, intend pouring tea into that old mug painted with medallions of a crowned king and queen? At the side of her own and Oliver's plates rested an ordinary cup and saucer.

Presently she scooped an extra faggot on to her son's rapidly emptied plate. 'Oliver,' she prattled absently, 'walked with Ivor to the farm to see the new sheepdog. A long walk!'

Prosser, in his stupor betraying the son whom he too admired, said with surprise: 'Ivor was in the Rising Sun with the sheepdog all the evening.'

Oliver bent over his faggot to hide his flush. Siân gave a squeezed-in laugh that made both father and son wince. 'I expect Oliver has started courting then,' she said. 'They often tell lies at first, as if they're doing something wrong.'

'I did go walking,' Oliver muttered, head still over his plate.

Prosser, more himself after food, began to spread himself. 'Is it Gwyneth Vaughan?' he boomed up to the beams. Going sententious, perhaps because he was a churchwarden of St. Teilo's and it was Sunday tomorrow, he rambled on: 'We all got to come to it. Man that is born of woman hath but a short time to live. He cometh up, and is cut down, like a—'

'Be quiet, Joseph Prosser!' his wife put a stop to this. 'Mixing up the funeral service with the marriage one!'

'I will keep my mouth as it were with a bridle,' he quoted further, however.

She rose and fetched the teapot from the hearth. Holding the pot high, but with a hand so accurately steady that the pouring seemed baleful, she filled the mug. The jet of dark tea descended to the mug long and thin as a whip. Prosser watched it go into the receptacle. Siân then walked round the table to her son. But he refused tea. He sat looking remote now, if not offended, and also not fully adjusted to whatever rankled within him. He got up. A waxen pallor had replaced the flush in his face. His mother did not question the unusual refusal of tea.

'I'm going to bed,' he mumbled.

He went to the dresser cupboard for his candlestick, lit it, and tramped up the stairs without another word, taking his mystery with him. Prosser sat with eyelids down, palms crossed over his stomach like a meditating monk, not touching the mug of tea. He waited until his son was safely in his room before saying, 'You've got to face it, Siân, my girl. You can't keep him to yourself for ever. I wonder is it Gwyneth Vaughan? She's always hanging round him in St. Teilo's.' It would be a desirable match. Gwyneth was sole offspring of a reasonably well-off family.

Siân assembled the table dishes. 'Gwyneth is a nice girl,' she said, in full approval. 'Aren't you going to drink your tea?'

'Don't hurry me, Siân,' he said, not looking at the mug.

She had taken two journeys with dishes to the kitchen before Oliver, candlestick still in hand, began to descend the stairs. His mother crossed to the table as though unnoticing. He put his feet down with slow care, stopped on the bottom stair, and asked: 'Where's my bed?'

'I burnt it,' his mother said, sugar basin in hand.

The only sound came from Prosser's scratching of his walnut-shell cheek. He stared fixedly at the mug again. Then the extraordinariness of the two events seemed to penetrate him with considerable force. 'Why have you burnt Oliver's bed?' he demanded, even aggressively. Oliver, sensing mysterious support, stood behind his candle, looking glassy as a young saint in a church window.

'Yes,' he said, though there was an under-squeak of dread in his voice, 'and where am I to sleep?'

Siân laid the sugar basin on the table, and spun round fast as a weathercock in a sudden blast of wind. She faced both the men in turn. 'That bed is burnt in the field!' she rapped out. 'And I've been to Catrin Morris's house tonight and knocked the wickedness out of *that* plotting old witch! See?' To her husband she exploded: 'Like mother, like daughter! And like father, like son! That daughter of Catrin's was in this house tonight! With *him*! But never again while I've got an ounce of strength to pull the trigger of your gun, Joseph Prosser...And you, Oliver,' she rasped to her overcome son, totally unlike the woman who purred in ministration to his every wish and need, 'no more from *you*! Get up to bed in the back room – and,' she added, 'don't forget to fall down on your knees by it and ask forgiveness…before you set foot in St. Teilo's tomorrow!' In a white surplice, perfectly starched and ironed by her, he sang a pure tenor in the choir.

The candle unsteady before him, Oliver returned up the stairs at once. A silence, bleak but seemly, followed Siân's outburst. Prosser moved from the table and the accusing mug. He unlaced his size eleven boots, bending from the armchair at his solidly-established hearth. Siân held out the painted mug to him.

'You haven't drunk your tea,' she said, with her pinched smile. 'You'll be thirsty in bed, after all those salty faggots.' She went off to the kitchen to wash up.

He drank the cooled tea with pondering slowness. The clock, flouting its heirloom age, ticked with a speedy clarity which always seemed to him mysteriously united with Siân's unwearied energy. Women, he ruminated, could seldom forget mischief done to them, however petty; and they had to be honoured; unlike men, they were unable to accept certain worldly matters with calm. Yet, as he remembered the gala Coronation Day of 1911, part of him seemed to become Siân. He experienced an approximation to her scorching fury on that day. That was what long marriage did to one, he thought: a bit one became like a woman.

Burning a good bed! But he experienced the drastic fury of that act too. He also heard a connecting explosion of fireworks. He remembered the laden tables in the meadow behind St.

Teilo's, the gay marquee, the barrels of strong ale, the games and competitions, the commemorative mugs, painted with the crowned heads, King George and Queen Mary, which were presented to every villager by Sir Llewellyn's wife on that 1911 afternoon. He remembered how, after dark had fallen, Catrin Morris had wheedled him—yes, wheedled him—into the copse below the meadow, when everybody's attention was on the opening of the fireworks display. He had been drunk by then, and it seemed only a minute before Siân had leapt in on them, snatched up Catrin's coronation mug from the grass, and smashed it to pieces on her red head. From where he lay, pushed over disregarded on the ground, he saw a soaring rocket burst into blue stars and fiery rain. He and Siân weren't married then, of course; only courting.

She came in from the kitchen, too briskly, and asked: 'Finished your tea?'

'Men,' he said, still pondering, 'they don't mean to do harm. They only get helpless in their nature. A man goes weak in the joints sometimes, and his mind goes dark...yes,' he brooded, 'dark'. He handed her the drained mug.

Her nose quivering over these obscurities, she observed: 'It's a good thing a woman stands watching from the other pan of the scales, then.'

Prosser continued to stare up at the pitted ceiling beams as he went on: 'Something there is that tells a man to take advantage of what's going.' He added, 'It's nothing serious, Siân.'

'What!' she exclaimed, thunderstruck.

be forced away from his grown-up darlings now? Just one more season of gathering, and, afterwards, he would be ready to decide about the future . . .

Then, remembering something else, he lamented, 'They'll come, they'll come!' They had such a special reason for making the journey. And this marooning snow would give even more urgency to their arguments regarding himself. He strained his keen old countryman's eyes down the anonymous white distances. Could they come? Could anyone break a way through those miles of deep snow, where nothing shuffled, crawled, or even flew? The whole world had halted. They would not come today. There would be one more day of peace.

Mesmerized at the window, he recalled another supreme time of snow, long ago, before he was married. He and two other farm workers had gone in search of Ambrose Owen's sheep. An old ram was found in a drift, stiff and upright on his legs, glassy eyes staring at nothing, curls of wool turned to a cockleshell hardness that could be chipped from the fleece. Farther away in the drift, nine wise ewes lay huddled against each other, and these were carried upside down by the legs to the farmhouse kitchen, where they thawed into life. But Ambrose, like that man in the Bible with a prodigal son, had broken down and shed tears over his lost ram that had foolishly wandered from the herd. The elderly farmer was in a low condition himself at the time, refusing to be taken to hospital, wanting to kick the bucket not only in his own home but downstairs in his fireside chair. Quite right too.

He returned from the window at last, drew a crimson

'Not in young men, Siân,' he said in some haste. 'Their heads are in the clouds and they can't see plainly what's going on below.'

'You mean,' she clarified for him, not displeased by this paternal concern, 'Oliver hasn't been wicked on purpose, bringing that fire-haired demon into the house. Well, I didn't say *he* was wicked. But *someone* had to fetch his head out of the clouds.'

'Well, you've put the fear of God into all concerned now, Siân.' He suppressed a belch, but managed to add, with some assertion of justice: 'She isn't a bad little whelp, on the whole, that girl isn't. But not suitable for Oliver, of course, of course.'

'Oh, go up to bed,' she said, only impatient, sure of her power in her own important territory.

I WILL KEEP HER COMPANY

When he achieved the feat of getting down the stairs to the icy living room, it was the peculiar silence there that impressed him. It had not been so noticeable upstairs, where all night he had had company, of a kind. Down in this room, the familiar morning sounds he had known for sixty years—all the crockery, pots and pans, and fire-grate noises of married life at break of day, his wife's brisk soprano not least among them—were abolished as though they had never existed.

It was the snow had brought this silence, of course. How many days had it been falling—four or five? He couldn't remember. Still dazed and stiff from his long vigil in a chair upstairs, he hobbled slowly to the window. Sight of the magnificent white spread brought, as always, astonishment. Who would have thought such a vast quantity waited above? Almighty in its power to obliterate the known works of man, especially his carefully mapped highways and byways, the weight of odourless substance was like a reminder that he was of no more account than an ant. But only a few last flakes were falling now, the small aster shapes drifting with dry languor on the hefty waves covering the long front garden.

'They'll be here today,' he said aloud, wakened a l[ittle] more by the dazzle. The sound of his voice was strange to h[im] like an echo of it coming back from a chasm. His head turn[ed] automatically towards the open door leading to the hallway, [and] broke the silence again, unwilling to let it settle. 'Been snow[ing] again all night, Maria. But it's stopping now. They'll come too[.] The roads have been blocked. Hasn't been a fall like it for years[.]'

His frosting breath plumed the air. He turned back to [the] window and continued to peer out for a while. A drift swelled [up] above the sill and there was no imprint of the robins and tits t[hat] regularly landed before the window in the morning, for break[fast] crumbs. Neither was there a sign of the garden gate into the la[ne] nor a glimpse of the village, two miles distant down the vall[ey] which could be seen from this height on green days. But [the] mountains, ramparts against howling Atlantic gales, were visible[,] glitteringly bleached outline against a pale-blue sky. Sava[ge] guardians of interior Wales, even their lowering black clouds a[nd] whipping rains were vanquished today. They looked innocent [in] their unbroken white.

His mind woke still more. The manacled landscape ga[ve] him, for the moment, a feeling of security. This snow was [a] protection, not a catastrophe. He did not want the overdue visito[rs] to arrive, did not want to exercise himself again in resistance [to] their arguments for his future welfare. Not yet. He thought of [the] six damson trees which he had introduced into the orchard a fe[w] years before and reared with such care. Last summer, there ha[d] been a nice little profit from the baskets of downy fruit. Was he [to]

flannel shawl from his sparsely-haired head, and re-arranged it carefully over his narrow shoulders. He wore two cardigans and trousers of thick home-spun, but the cold penetrated to his bones. Still unwilling to begin the day's ritual of living down in this room, he stood gazing vaguely from the cinder-strewn fireplace to the furniture, his eyes lingering on the beautifully polished rosewood table at which, with seldom a cross word exchanged (so it seemed now), he had shared good breakfasts for a lifetime. Was it because of the unnatural silence, with not the whirr of a single bird outside, that all the familiar contents of the room seemed withdrawn from ownership. They looked stranded.

Remembrance came to him of the room having this same hush of unbelonging when he and Maria had first walked into it, with the idea of buying the place, a freehold stone cottage and its four acres, for ninety-five sovereigns, cash down. They were courting at the time, and the property was cheap because of its isolation; no one had lived there for years. The orchard, still well-stocked, had decided him, and Maria, who could depend on herself and a husband for all the talking she needed, agreed because of the tremendous views of mountain range and sky from this closed end of the valley. What a walker she had been! Never wanted even a bike, did not want to keep livestock, and was content with the one child that came very soon after the rushed purchase of the cottage. But, disregarding gossip, she had liked to go down to church in the village, where she sang psalms louder than any other woman there.

He had huddled closer into the shawl. Since he would not

be staying long down here, was it worthwhile lighting a fire? Then he realized that if the visitors found means of coming, it would be prudent to let them see he could cope with the household jobs. First, the grate to be raked, and a fire laid; wood and coal to be fetched from outside, but he couldn't hurry. His scalp was beginning to prickle and contract, and he drew the shawl over his head again. Feeling was already gone from his feet when he reached the shadowy kitchen lying off the living room, fumblingly pulled the back door open, and faced a wall of pure white.

The entire door space was blocked, sealing access to the shed in which, besides wood and coal, oil for the cooking stove was stored. He had forgotten that the wall had been there the day before. Snow had drifted down the mountain slope and piled as far as the back window upstairs even then; it came back to him that he had drawn the kitchen window curtains to hide that weight of tombstone white against the panes. 'Marble,' he said now, curiously running a finger over the crisply hardened surface. He shut the door, relieved that one item in the morning jobs was settled; it would be impossible to reach the shed from the front of the cottage.

Pondering in the dowdy light of the kitchen, he looked at the empty glass oil-feeder of the cooking stove, at the empty kettle, at an earthenware pitcher, which he knew was empty too. He remembered that the water butt against the outside front wall had been frozen solid for days before the snow began. And even if he had the strength to dig a path to the well in the orchard, very likely that would be frozen. Would snow melt inside the house? But a little water remained in a ewer upstairs. And wasn't there still some of the milk that the district nurse had brought? He found the jug in the slate-shelved larder, and tilted it; the inch-deep, semi-congealed liquid moved. He replaced the jug with a wrinkling nose, and peered at the three tins of soup that also had been brought by Nurse Baldock.

Sight of the tins gave him a feeling of nausea. The last time the nurse had come—*which* day was it? —a smell like ammonia had hung about her. And her pink rubber gloves, her apron with its row of safety pins and a tape measure dangling over it, had badly depressed him. A kind woman, though, except for her deciding what was the best way for a man to live. The sort that treated all men as little boys. She had a voice that wouldn't let go of a person, but being a woman, a soft wheedling could come into it when she chose. Thank God the snow had bogged her down.

He reached for a flat box, opened it, and saw a few biscuits. Maria always liked the lid picture of Caernarfon Castle, which they'd visited one summer day; he looked at it now with a reminiscent chuckle. His movements became automatically exact, yet vague and random. He found a tin tray inscribed 'Ringer's Tobacco' and placed on it the box, a plate and, forgetting there was no milk left upstairs, a clean cup and saucer. This done, he suddenly sat down on a hard chair and closed his eyes.

He did not know how long he remained there. Tapping sounds roused him; he jerked from the chair with galvanized strength. Agitation gave his shouts an unreasonable cantankerousness as he reached the living room. 'They've come! Open the door, can't you? It's not locked.'

He opened the front door. There was nobody. The snow reached up to his waist, and the stretch of it down the garden slope bore not a mark. Only an elephant could come to this door. Had he dreamed the arrival? Or had a starving bird tapped its beak on the window? The dread eased. He shut the door with both his shaking hands, and stood listening in the small hallway. 'They haven't come!' he shouted up the stairs, wanting to hear his voice smashing the silence. 'But they will, they will! They are bringing my pension money from the post office. Dr. Howells took my book with him.' Self-reminder of this ordinary matter helped to banish the dread, and the pain in his chest dwindled.

Pausing in the living room, he remembered that it was actually Nurse Baldock who had taken his book and put it in that important black bag of hers. She had arrived that day with Dr. Howells in his car, instead of on her bike. The snow had begun to fall, but she said it wouldn't be much—only a sprinkling. And Dr. Howells had told him not to worry and that everything would be put in hand. But even the doctor, who should have had a man's understanding, had argued about the future, and coaxed like Nurse Baldock. Then she had said she'd bring Vicar Pryce on her next visit. People fussing! But he couldn't lock the door against them yet. It was necessary for them to come just once again. He would pretend to listen to them, especially the vicar, and when they had gone he would lock the door, light a fire, and sit down to think of the future in his own way.

His eyes strayed about the room again. He looked at the table with its green-shaded oil lamp, at the dresser with its display of brilliant plates and lustre jugs, at the comfortable low chairs, the bright rugs, the scroll-backed sofa from which Maria had directed his activities for the week before she was obliged to take to her bed at last. After the shock of the fancied arrival, the objects in the room no longer seemed withdrawn from ownership. They would yield him security and ease, for a long while yet. And the cooking stove in the kitchen, the pans, brooms and brushes—they had belonged solely to Maria's energetic hands, but after a lifetime with her he knew exactly how she dealt with them. Any man with three penn'orth of sense could live here independently as a lord. Resolve lay tucked away in his mind. Today, with this cold stunning his senses, not much could be done. He must wait. His eyes reached the mantelpiece clock; lifting the shawl from his ears, he stared closer at the age-yellowed face. *That* was why the silence had been so strange! Was even a clock affected by the cold? Surely he had wound it last night, as usual; surely he had come downstairs? The old-fashioned clopping sound, steady as horse hoofs ambling on a quiet country road, had never stopped before. The defection bothering him more than the lack of means for a fire and oil for the stove, he reached for the mahogany-framed clock, his numb fingers moving over it to take a firm grip. It fell into the stoneflagged hearth. There was a tinkle of broken glass.

'Ah,' he shouted guiltily, 'the clock's broken, Maria! Slipped out of my hand!'

He gazed at it in a stupor. But the accident finally decided him. Down in this room the last bits of feeling were ebbing from him. There was warmth and company upstairs. He stumbled into the kitchen, lifted the tin tray in both hands without feeling its substance, and reached the hallway. Negotiation of the stairs took even more time than his descent had. As in the kitchen, it was the propulsion of old habit that got him up the flight he had climbed thousands of times. The tray fell out of his hands when he reached a squeaking stair just below the landing. This did not matter; he even liked the lively explosion of noise. 'It's only that advertisement tray the shop gave you one Christmas!' he called out, not mentioning the crocks and biscuit box which had crashed to the bottom. He did not attempt to retrieve anything. All he wanted was warmth.

In the clear white light of a front room he stood for some moments looking intently at the weather-browned face of the small woman lying on a four-poster bed. Her eyes were compactly shut. Yet her face bore an expression of prim vigour; still she looked alert in her withdrawal. No harsh glitter of light from the window reached her, but he drew a stiff fold of the gay-patterned linen bed curtains that, as if in readiness for this immurement, had been washed, starched and ironed by her three weeks before. Then he set about his own task. The crimson shawl still bonneted his head.

His hands plucked at the flannel blankets and larger shawls lying scattered on the floor around a wheelbacked armchair close to the bed. Forcing grip into his fingers, he draped these coverings methodically over the sides and back of the chair, sat down, and swathed his legs and body in the overlapping folds. It all took a long time, and for a while it brought back the pain in his chest, compelling him to stop. Finally, he succeeded in drawing portions of two other shawls over his head and shoulders, so that he was completely encased in draperies. There had been good warmth in this cocoon last night. The everlasting flannel was woven in a mill down the valley, from the prized wool of local mountain sheep. Properly washed in rain water, it yielded warmth for a hundred years or more. There were old valley people who had been born and had gone in the same pair of handed-down family blankets.

Secure in the shelter, he waited patiently for warmth to come. When it began to arrive, and the pain went, his mind flickered into activity again. It was of the prancing mountain ponies he thought first, the wild auburn ponies that were so resentful of capture. He had always admired them. But what did their lucky freedom mean now? *They* had no roof over their head, and where could they find victuals? Had they lost their bearings up in their fastnesses? Were they charging in demented panic through the endless snow, plunging into crevices, starvation robbing them of instinct and sense? Then there were the foxes. He remembered hearing during that drastic time of snow when he rescued Ambrose Owen's sheep, a maddened fox had dashed into the vicarage kitchen when a servant opened the back door. It snatched in its teeth a valuable Abyssinian cat lying fast asleep on the hearth rug, and streaked out before the petrified woman could scream.

A little more warmth came. He crouched into it with a

sigh. Soon it brought a sense of summer pleasures. A long meadow dotted with buttercups and daisies shimmered before him, and a golden-haired boy ran excitedly over the bright grass to a young white goat tied to an iron stake. Part of the meadow was filled with booths of striped canvas, and a roundabout of painted horses galloped to barrel-organ music. It was that Whitsuntide fete when he had won the raffled goat on a sixpenny ticket—the only time he had won anything all his life. Maria had no feeling for goats, especially rams, but she had let their boy lead the snowy-haired beast home. Richard had looked after it all its sturdy years and, at its hiring, got for himself the fees of its natural purpose in life—five shillings a time, in those far-off days.

The father chuckled. He relaxed further in the dark chair. His hands resting lightly on his knees, he prepared for sleep. It was slow in taking him, and when, drowsily, he heard a whirring sound he gave it no particular attention. But he stirred slightly and opened his eyes. The noise approached closer. It began to circle, now faint, then loud, now dwindling. He did not recognize it. It made him think of a swarm of chirping grasshoppers, then of the harsh clonking of roused geese. Neutral towards all disturbance from outside, he nestled deeper into the warmth bred of the last thin heat of his blood, and when a louder noise shattered the peace of his cocoon he still did not move, though his eyes jerked wide open once more.

The helicopter circled twice above the half-buried cottage. Its clacking sounded more urgent as it descended and began to pass as low as the upstairs windows at the front and back. The noise became a rasp of impatience, as if the machine were annoyed that no reply came to this equivalent of a knocking on the door, that no attention was paid to the victory of this arrival. A face peered down from a curved grey pane; the head of another figure dodged behind, moving to both the side panels.

Indecision seemed to govern this hovering above the massed billows of snow. After the cottage had been circled three times, the machine edged nearer the front wall, and a square box wrapped in orange-coloured oilskin tumbled out, fell accurately before the door, and lay visible in a hole of snow. The machine rose; its rotor blades whirled for seconds above the cottage before it mounted higher. It diminished into the pale afternoon light, flying down from the valley towards immaculate mountains that had never known a visit from such a strange bird.

Evening brought an unearthly blue to the sculptured distances. Night scarcely thickened the darkness; the whiteness could be seen for miles. Only the flashing of clear-cut stars broke the long stillness of the valley. No more snow fell. But the cold hardened during the low hours, and at dawn, though a red glow lay in the sun's disc on Moelwyn's crest, light came with grudging slowness, and there was no promise of thaw all morning. But, soon after the sun had passed the zenith, another noise smashed into the keep of silence at the valley's closed end.

Grinding and snorting, a vehicle slowly burrowed into the snow. It left in its wake, like a gigantic horned snail, a silvery track, on which crawled a plain grey motor van. Ahead, the climbing plough was not once defeated by its pioneering work, thrusting past shrouded hedges on either side of it, its grunting front mechanism churning up the snow and shooting it out of a curved-over horn on to bushes at the left. The attendant grey van stopped now and then, allowing a measure of distance to accumulate on the smooth track.

The van had three occupants. Two of them, sitting on the driver's cushioned bench, were philosophically patient of this laborious journeying. The third, who was Nurse Baldock, squatted on the floor inside the small van, her legs stretched towards the driver's seat and her shoulders against the back door. She was a substantial woman, and the ungainly fur coat she wore gave her the dimensions of a mature bear. She tried not to be restless. But as the instigator of this rescuing operation, she kept looking at her watch, and she failed to curb herself all the time. The two men in front had not been disposed for talk.

'I hope that thing up there won't break down,' she said presently. 'It's a Canadian snowplough—so I was told on the phone. The Council bought it only last year.'

'It took them a deuce of a time to get one after we had that nasty snowfall in 1947,' remarked the driver, a middle-aged man in a sombre vicuna overcoat and a bowler hat. 'A chap and his young lady were found buried in their car halfway up Moelwyn when we had *that* lot—been there a week, if you remember, Vicar. Thank God these bad falls don't come often.'

'Councils seldom look far outside their town hall chamber after election,' mumbled Vicar Pryce, who had been picked up in

Ogwen village twenty minutes earlier. Under his round black hat only his eyes and bleak nose were visible from wrappings of scarves. It was very cold in the utilitarian van, lent for this emergency expedition by a tradesman of the market town at the valley's mouth; the road from there to Ogwen had been cleared the day before.

'Well, our Council has got hold of a helicopter this time, too,' Nurse Baldock reminded them, not approving of criticism of her employers from anyone. 'Soon as I heard they had hired one to drop bundles of hay to stranded cattle and mountain ponies, I said to myself, "Man first, then the beasts," and flew to my phone. I'm fond of old John Evans, though he's so wilful. I arranged to have tins of food, fruit juice, milk, a small bottle of brandy, fresh pork sausages, and bread put in the box, besides a plastic container of cooker oil and a message from me.'

'Couldn't you have gone in the helicopter?' the driver asked, rather inattentively.

'What, and got dropped out into the snow with the box?' The nurse's bulk wobbled with impatience. 'If the machine couldn't land anywhere on those deep slopes of snow, how could I get down, I ask you?'

'I thought they could drop a person on a rope.' The driver sounded propitiatory now. For him, as for most people, the district nurse was less a woman than a portent of inescapable forces lying in wait for everybody.

'Delivery of necessities was the point,' she said dismissingly, and, really for Vicar Pryce's wrapped ears, continued,

'After getting the helicopter man's report yesterday, I was on the phone to the Town Hall for half an hour. I insisted that they let me have the snowplough today—I *fought* for it. It was booked for this and that, they said, but I had my way in the end.'

'Last night was bitter,' Vicar Pryce said, following a silence, 'I got up at 3 a.m. and piled a sheepskin floor rug on my bed.'

'Bitter it *was*,' agreed Nurse Baldock. 'We single people feel it the more.' Neither of the men offered a comment, and, with another look at her watch, she pursued, 'Of course, the helicopter man's report needn't mean a lot. Who could blame Evans if he stayed snuggled in bed all day? And at his age, he could sleep through any noise.'

'One would think a helicopter's clatter would bring him out of any sleep, Nurse,' the Vicar remarked.

'I think he's a bit deaf,' she replied, rejecting the doubt. 'In any case, I don't suppose he'd know what the noise meant.' The van stopped, and she decided, 'We'll have our coffee now.'

She managed to spread quite a picnic snack on the flat top of a long, calico-covered object lying beside her, on which she wouldn't sit. There were cheese and egg sandwiches, pieces of sultana cake, plates, mugs, sugar and a large Thermos flask. A heavy can of paraffin propped her back, and, in addition to the satchel of picnic stuff, she had brought her official leather bag, well known in the valley. Nurse Baldock's thoroughness was as dreaded by many as was sight of her black bag. After determined efforts over several years, she had recently been awarded a social science diploma, and now, at forty-five, she hoped for a more important position than that of a bicycle-borne district nurse. This rescuing mission today would help prove her mettle, and Vicar Pryce, to whom she had insisted on yielding the seat in front, would be a valuable witness of her zeal.

'I'll keep enough for the young man in the snowplough,' she said, pouring coffee. 'He ought not to stop now. The quicker we get there the better.'

'Makes one think of places on the moon,' the driver remarked, gazing out at the waxen countryside.

Sipping coffee, she resumed, 'I have eight patients in Ogwen just now, and I really ought not to be spending all this time on a man who's got nothing the matter with him except old age and obstinacy. Two confinements due any day now.' The men drank and ate, and she added, 'What a time for births! There's Mavis Thomas, for instance—she's not exactly entitled to one, is she, Vicar? But at least that man she lives with keeps her house on Sheep's Gap warm, and her water hasn't frozen.'

'Nobody except a choirboy turned up for matins last Sunday,' the meditative vicar said. 'So I cancelled all services that day.'

Nurse Baldock finished a piece of cake. 'I heard yesterday that a married woman living up on Sheep's Gap was chased by two starving ponies that found a way down from the mountains. You know how they won't go near human beings as a rule, but when this woman came out of her farmhouse in her gumboots they stampeded from behind a barn; with their teeth grinding and eyes flaring. She ran back screaming into the house just in time.'

'Perhaps she was carrying a bucket of pig feed and they smelt it,' the driver suggested, handing back his mug.

Undeterred, Nurse Baldock gave a feminine shiver. 'I keep an eye open for them on my rounds. We might be back in the days of wolves.' The van resumed its amble on the pearly track as she proceeded. 'But these are modern times. Old Evans would never dream he would get a helicopter for his benefit, to say nothing of that great ugly thing in front, *and* us. There's real Christianity for you! This affair will cost the Council quite a sum. It will go on the rates, of course.'

'John and Maria Evans,' Vicar Pryce said, rewrapping his ears in the scarves, 'were always faithful parishioners of mine when they were able to get down to the village. I remember their son Richard, too. A good tenor in the choir. Emigrated to New Zealand and has children of his own there, I understand.'

'Well, Vicar,' Nurse Baldock said, packing the crocks into the satchel between her knees, 'I hope you'll do your very best to persuade Evans to leave with us today and go to Pistyll Mawr Home. Heaven knows, I did all I could to coax him when I was at the cottage with Dr. Howells the other day.'

'It will be a business,' he mumbled.

She pursed her lips. 'He told me it was healthy up there in his cottage, and that he and his wife had always liked the views. "Views!" I said, "Views won't feed and nurse you if you fall ill. Come now, facts must be faced." Then he said something about his damson trees. I told him Pistyll Mawr had fruit trees in plenty.'

The driver, who lived in the market town, spoke. 'Don't the new cases take offence at being forced to have a bath as soon as they enter the doors of Pistyll Mawr?'

'So you've heard that one, have you? Why, what's wrong with a bath? Is it a crime?' Nurse Baldock had bridled. 'I am able to tell you there's a woman in Pistyll Mawr who brags about her baths there—says that for the first time in her life she feels like a well-off lady, with a maid to sponge her back and hand her a towel. You're out of date, sir, with your "take offence".'

'Aren't there separate quarters for men and women, even if they're married?' he persisted.

'As if very elderly people are bothered by what you mean! Besides, they can flirt in the garden if they want. But old people have too much dignity for such nonsense.'

'I dare say there are one or two exceptions.'

'Ah, I agree there.' Nurse Baldock pulled gauntlet gloves over her mittens. 'The aged! They're our biggest problem. The things that come my way from some of them! One has to have nerves of iron, and it doesn't do to let one's eyes fill. Why must people trouble themselves so much about the young? My blood boils when I see all the rubbishy fuss made about the youngsters by newspapers and busybodies of the lay public. Sight of the word "teenagers" makes me want to throw up. Leave the young alone, I say! They've got all the treasures of the world on their backs, and once they're out of school they don't put much expense on the rates.'

After this tirade no one spoke for a time. As the van

crawled nearer the valley's majestic closure, Nurse Baldock herself seemed to become oppressed by the solemn desolation outside. Not a boulder or streak of path showed on Moelwyn's swollen heights. Yet, close at hand, there were charming snow effects. The van rounded a turn of the lane, and breaks in the hedges on either side revealed birch glades, their spectral depths glittering as though from the light of ceremonial chandeliers. All the crystal-line birches were struck into eternal stillness—fragile, rime-heavy boughs sweeping downward, white hairs of mourning. Not a bird, rabbit, or beetle could stir in those frozen grottoes, and the blue harebell or the pink convolvulus never ring out in them again.

'Up here doesn't seem to belong to us,' Vicar Pryce said, when the van halted again. 'It's the white. If only we could see just one little robin hopping about the branches! The last time I came this way, I saw pheasants crossing the roads and then they rose. Such colour! It was soon after Easter, and the windflowers and primroses were out.'

'We might be travelling in a wheelbarrow,' sighed Nurse Baldock, as the van moved. She looked at her watch, then into her official bag, and said, 'I've got Evans's old-age pension money. Because of his wife's taking to her bed, he worried about not being able to leave the cottage. I told him, "You're lucky you've got someone like me to look after you, but it's not my bounden task to collect your pension money, Council-employed though I am. Things can't go on like this, my dear sir, come now".'

'You've been kind to him,' the Vicar acknowledged at last.

'It's the State that is kind,' she said stoutly. 'We can say there's no such thing as neglect or old-fashioned poverty for the elderly now. But in my opinion the lay public has begun to take our welfare schemes too much for granted. The other day, I was able to get a wig free of charge for a certain madam living not a hundred miles from this spot, and when I turned up with it on my bike she complained it wasn't the right brown shade and she couldn't wear it—a woman who is not able to step outside her door and is seventy-eight!'

'The aged tend to cling to their little cussednesses,' Vicar Pryce mumbled, in a lacklustre way.

'Yes, indeed.' They were nearing their destination now, and Nurse Baldock, tenacity unabated, seized her last opportunity. 'But do press the real advantages of Pistyll Mawr Home to Evans, Vicar. We are grateful when the Church does its share in these cases. After all, my concern is with the body.' This earned no reply, and she said, 'Germs! It's too icy for them to be active just now, but with the thaw there'll be a fine crop of bronchials and influenzas, mark my words! And I don't relish coming all this way to attend to Evans if he's struck down, probably through not taking proper nourishment.' There was a further silence, and she added, 'On the other hand, these outlying cases ought to convince the Health Department that I must be given a car—don't you agree, Vicar?'

'I wonder you have not had one already. Dr. Howells should—'

A few yards ahead, the plough had stopped. Its driver leaned out of his cabin and yelled, 'Can't see a gate!'

'I'll find it,' Nurse Baldock declared.

The vicar and van driver helped to ease her out of the back doors. She shook her glut of warm skirts down, and clumped forward in her gumboots. A snow-caked roof and chimney could be seen above a billowing white slope. Scanning the contours of a buried hedge, the nurse pointed. 'The gate is there. I used to lean my bike against that tree.' It was another lamenting birch, the crystal-entwined branches drooped to the snow.

The plough driver, an amiable-looking young man in an elegant alpine sweater, brought out three shovels. Nurse Baldock scolded him for not having four. Valiantly, when he stopped for coffee and sandwiches, she did a stint, and also used the Vicar's shovel while he rested. They had shouted towards the cottage. There was no response and, gradually, they ceased to talk. It took them half an hour to clear a way up the garden. They saw the oil-skin wrapped box as they neared the door. The nurse, her square face professionally rid of comment now, had already fetched her bag.

It was even colder in the stone house than outside. Nurse Baldock, the first to enter, returned from a swift trot into the living room and kitchen to the men clustered in the little hallway. She stepped to the staircase. All-seeing as an investigating policewoman, she was nevertheless respecting the social decencies. Also, despite the sight of broken crockery, a biscuit box, and a tray scattered below the stairs, she was refusing to face defeat yet. 'John Ormond Evans,' she called up, 'are you there?' Her voice had the challenging ring sometimes used for encouraging the declining back to the world of health, and after a moment of silence, she added, with an unexpected note of entreaty, 'The vicar is here!' The three men, like awkward intruders in a private place, stood listening. Nurse Baldock braced herself. 'Come up with me,' she whispered.

Even the plough driver followed her. But when the flannel wrappings were stripped away, John Ormond Evans sat gazing out at them from his chair as though in mild surprise at this intrusion into his comfortable retreat. His deep-sunk blue eyes were frostily clear under arched white brows. He looked like one awakened from restorative slumber, an expression of judicious independence fixed on his spare face. His hands rested on his knees, like a Pharaoh's.

Nurse Baldock caught in her breath with a hissing sound. The two older men, who had remained hatted and gloved in the icy room, stood dumbly arrested. It was the ruddy-cheeked young man who suddenly put out a bare, instinctive hand and, with a movement of extraordinary delicacy, tried to close the blue eyes. He failed.

'I closed my father's eyes,' he stammered, drawing away in bashful apology for his strange temerity.

'Frozen,' pronounced Vicar Pryce, removing his round black hat. He seemed about to offer a few valedictory words.

Nurse Baldock pulled herself together. She swallowed, and said, 'Lack of nourishment, too!' She took off a gauntlet glove, thrust fingers round one of the thin wrists for a token feel, and then stepped back. 'Well, here's a problem! Are we to take him back with us?'

Vicar Pryce turned to look at the woman lying on the curtain-hung bed. Perhaps because his senses were blurred by the cold, he murmured, 'She's very small—smaller than I remember her. Couldn't he go in the coffin with her for the journey back?'

'No,' said Nurse Baldock promptly. 'He couldn't be straightened here.'

The van driver, an auxiliary assistant in busy times to Messrs Eccles, the market-town undertakers, confirmed, 'Set, set.'

'As he was in his ways!' burst from Nurse Baldock in her chagrin. 'This needn't have happened if he had come with me, as I wanted six days ago! Did he sit there all night deliberately?'

It was decided to take him. The coffin, three days late in delivery, was fetched from the van by the driver and the young man. Maria Evans, aged eighty-three, and prepared for this journey by the nurse six days before, by no means filled its depth and length. Gone naturally, of old age, and kept fresh by the cold, she looked ready to rise punctiliously to meet the face of the Almighty with the same hale energy as she had met each washing day on earth. Her shawl-draped husband, almost equally small, was borne out after her in his sitting posture. Nurse Baldock, with the Vicar for witness, locked up the house. Already it had an air of not belonging to anyone. 'We must tell the police we found the clock lying broken in the hearth,' she said. 'There'll be an inquest, of course.'

John Evans, head resting against the van's side, travelled

sitting on his wife's coffin; Vicar Pryce considered it unseemly for him to be laid on the floor. The helicopter box of necessities and the heavy can of oil, placed on either side of him, held him secure. Nurse Baldock chose to travel with the young man in the draughty cabin of his plough. Huddled in her fur coat, and looking badly in need of her own hearth, she remained sunk in morose silence now.

The plough, no longer spouting snow, trundled in the van's rear. 'Pretty in there!' the driver ventured to say, in due course. They were passing the spectral birch glades. A bluish shade had come to the depths.

Nurse Baldock stirred. Peering out, she all but spat. 'Damned, damned snow! All my work wasted! Arguments on the phone, a helicopter, and this plough! The cost! I shall have to appear before the Health Committee.'

'I expect they'll give you credit for all you've done for the old fellow,' said the driver, also a Council employee.

She was beyond comforting just then. 'Old people won't *listen*! When I said to him six days ago, "Come with me, there's nothing you can do for her now," he answered, "Not yet. I will keep her company." I could have taken him at once to Pistyll Mawr Home. It was plain he couldn't look after himself. One of those unwise men who let themselves be spoilt by their wives.'

'Well, they're not parted now,' the young man said.

'The point is, if he had come with me he would be enjoying a round of buttered toast in Pistyll Mawr at this very moment. I blame myself for not trying hard enough. But how was I to know all this damn snow was coming?'

'A lot of old people don't like going into Pistyll Mawr Home, do they?'

'What's wrong with Pistyll Mawr? Hetty Jarvis, the matron, has a heart of gold. What's more, now I've got my social science diploma, I'm applying for her position when she retires next year.'

'Good luck to you.' The driver blew on his hands. Already, the speedier van had disappeared into the whiteness.

'The lay public,' Nurse Baldock sighed, looking mollified, '*will* cling to its prejudices.' And half to herself, she went on, 'Hetty Jarvis complained to me that she hasn't got anything like enough inmates to keep her staff occupied. "Baldock," she said to me, "I'm depending on you," and I phoned her only this week to say I had found someone for her, a sober and clean man I would gamble had many years before him if he was properly cared for.'

'Ah,' murmured the driver. He lit a cigarette, at which his preoccupied passenger—after all, they were in a kind of funeral—frowned.

'People should see the beeswaxed parquet floors in Pistyll Mawr,' she pursued. 'When the hydrangeas are in bloom along the drive, our Queen herself couldn't wish for a better approach to her home. The bishop called it a noble sanctuary in his opening-day speech. And so it is!'

'I've heard the Kingdom of Heaven is like that,' the young man remarked idly. 'People have got to be pushed in.'

Nurse Baldock turned to look at his round face, to which had come, perhaps because of the day's rigours, the faint purple hue of a ripening fig. 'You might think differently later on, my boy,' she commented in a measured way. 'I can tell you there comes a time when few of us are able to stand alone. You saw today what resulted for one who made the wrong choice.'

'Oh, I don't know. I expect he knew what he was doing, down inside him.'

She sighed again, apparently patient of ignorance and youthful lack of feeling. 'I was fond of old Evans,' she said.

'Anyone can see it,' he allowed.

She remained silent for a long while. The costly defeat continued to weigh on her until the plough had lumbered on to the flat of the valley's bed. There, she looked at her watch and began to bustle up from melancholy. 'Five hours on this one case!' she fidgeted. 'I ought to have gone back in the van. I'm due at a case up on Sheep's Gap.'

'Another old one?'

'No, thank God. An illegitimate maternity. Not the first one for her either! And I've got another in the row of cottages down by the little waterfall—a legitimate.' The satisfaction of a life-giving smack on the bottom seemed to resound in her perked-up voice. 'We need them more than ever in nasty times like these, don't we? Providing a house is warm and well stocked for the welcome. Can't you make this thing go faster?'

'I'm at top speed. It's not built for maternities of any kind.'

Nurse Baldock sniffed. She sat more benevolently, however, and offered from the official black bag a packet of barley-sugar sweets. The village lay less than a mile distant. But it was some time before there was a sign of natural life out in the white purity. The smudged outline of a church tower and clustering houses had come into view when the delighted young man exclaimed, 'Look!' Arriving from nowhere, a hare had jumped on to the smooth track. His jump lacked a hare's usual celerity. He seemed bewildered, and sat up for an instant, ears tensed to the noise breaking the silence of these chaotic acres, a palpitating eye cast back in assessment of the oncoming plough. Then his forepaws gave a quick play of movement, like shadowboxing, and he sprang forward on the track with renewed vitality. Twice he stopped to look as though in need of affiliation with the plough's motion. But, beyond a bridge over the frozen rivers he took a flying leap and, paws barely touching the hardened snow and scut whisking, escaped out of sight.

THE FASHION PLATE

'The Fashion Plate's coming—' Quickly the news would pass down the main road. Curtains twitched in front parlour windows, potted shrubs were moved or watered; some colliers' wives, hard-worked and canvas-aproned, came boldly out to the doorsteps to stare. In the dingy little shops, wedged here and there among the smart dwellings, customers craned together for the treat. Cleopatra setting out in the golden barge to meet Antony did not create more interest. There was no one else in the valley like her. Her hats! The fancy high-heeled shoes, the brilliantly elegant dresses in summer, the tweeds and the swirl of furs for the bitter days of that mountainous district! The different handbags, gay and sumptuous, the lacy gloves, the parasols and tasselled umbrellas! And how she knew how to wear these things! Graceful as a swan, clean as a flower, she dazzled the eye.

But, though a pleasure to see, she was also incongruous, there in that grim industrial retreat pushed up among the mountains, with the pits hurling out their clouds of grit, and clanking coal-wagons crossing the main road twice, and the miners coming off the shift black and primitive-looking. The women drew in their breaths as she passed. She looked as if she had never done a stroke of work in her life. Strange murmurs could be heard; she almost created a sense of fear, this vision of delicate indolence, wealth and taste assembled with exquisite tact in one person. How could she do it? Their eyes admired but their comments did not.

Yet the work-driven women of this place, that had known long strikes, bitter poverty and a terrible pit disaster, could not entirely malign Mrs. Mitchell. Something made them pause. Perhaps it was the absolute serenity of those twice-weekly afternoon walks that nothing except torrential rain or snow-bound roads could prevent. Or perhaps they saw a vicarious triumph of themselves, a dream become courageously real.

There remained the mystery of how she could afford all those fine clothes. For Mrs. Mitchell was only the wife of the man in charge of the slaughter-house. She was not the pit manager's wife (indeed, Mrs. Edwards dressed in a totally different style, her never-varied hat shaped like an Eskimo's hut). Mr. Mitchell's moderate salary was known, and in such a place no one could possess private means without it being exact knowledge. Moreover, he was no match to his wife. A rough and ready sort of man, glum and never mixing much in the life of the place, though down in the slaughter-house, which served all the butcher shops for miles, he was respected as a responsible chap whose words and deed were to be trusted. Of words he had not many.

The women wished they could curl their tongues round something scandalous. Why was Mrs. Mitchell always having her photograph taken buy Mr. Burgess in his studio down an obscure yard where he worked entirely alone? But nobody felt that suspicion of Mr. Burgess, a family man and a chapel deacon with a stark knobbly face above a high stiff collar, sat comfortably in the mind. The bit of talk about the two had started because one afternoon a mother calling at the studio to fix an appointment for her daughter's wedding party found Mrs. Mitchell reclining on a sofa under a bust of Napoleon. She was hatless and, in a clinging dress ('tight on her as a snake-skin') and her hand holding a bunch of artificial flowers, she looked like a woman undergoing the agonies of some awful confession. Mr. Burgess certainly had his head under the black drapery of his camera, so everything pointed to yet another photograph being taken. But to have one taken *lying down*! In the valley, in those days, to have a photo taken was a rare event attended by tremendous fuss. Accompanied by advising friends or relations, one stood up to the ordeal as if going before the Ultimate Judge, and one always came out on the card as if turned to stone or a pillar of salt.

The whispering began. Yet still everyone felt that the whispering was unfair to Mr. Burgess. For thirty years he had photographed wedding parties, oratorio choirs and silver cup football teams in his studio, and nothing had ever been said against his conduct.

Mrs. Mitchell, coming out of her bow-windowed little house as out of a palace, took her walks as if never a breath of scandal ever polluted her pearl earrings Was she aware of the general criticism? If so, did she know that within the criticism was homage?—the homage that in bygone times would begin a dynasty of tribal queens? Was she aware of the fear too, the puritanic dread that such lavishness and extravagance could not be obtained but at some dire cost greater even than money?

II

This afternoon her excursion was no different from the hundreds of others. It was a fine autumn day. The tawny mountains glistened like the skins of lions. She wore a new fur, rich with the bluish-black tint of grapes, and flung with just the right expensive carelessness across her well-held shoulders: it would cause additional comment. With her apparently unaware look of repose she passed serenely down the long drab main road.

Down at the bottom of the valley the larger shops, offices, a music-hall and a railway station (together with Mr. Burgess's studio) clustered into the semblance of a town. She always walked as far as the railway station, situated down a hunch-backed turning, and, after appearing to be intent on its architecture for a moment, wheeled round and with a mysterious smile began the homeward journey. Often she made small domestic purchases—her clothes she obtained from the city twenty miles away—and as the ironmonger's wife once remarked: 'Only a rolling-pin she wanted, but one would think she was buying a grand piano.'

Today, outside the railway station, she happened to see her young friend Nicholas and, bending down to his ear, in her low sweet voice breathed his name. He was twelve, wore a school satchel strapped to his back, and he was absentmindedly paused before a poster depicting Windsor Castle. He gave a violent start and dropped a purple-whorled glass marble which rolled across the pavement, sped down the gutter and slid into a drain— 'It's gone!'

he cried in poignant astonishment. 'I won it dinner-time!'

'And all my fault.' Her bosom was perfumed with an evasive fragrance like closed flowers. 'Never mind, *I* have some marbles—will you come and get them this evening? You've been neglecting us lately, Nicholas.' She was neither arch nor patronising; he might have been a successful forty.

'I'll have to do my homework first,' he said with equal formality.

'Well, come in and do it with us. You shall have your own little table, and I'll be quiet as a mouse.'

They lived in the same street and though no particular friendship existed between the two households, he had been on visiting terms with the Mitchells, who were childless, for a couple of years. The change from his own noisily warring brothers'-and-sisters' home to the Mitchells', where he was sole little king, nourished him. To his visits his mother took a wavering attitude of doubt, half criticism and compassion; before becoming decisive she was waiting for something concrete to happen in that house.

That evening Mrs. Mitchell had six coloured glass marbles ready for him on a small table on which also, neatly set out, were a crystal ink-well, a ruler, blotter and pencils and . . . yes! a bottle of lemonade with a tumbler. Very impressed by the bottle, which gave him a glimpse of easy luxury in a world hard with the snatching and blows of his brothers and sisters, he made little fuss of the glitteringly washed marbles, which he guessed she had bought in Watkins's shop after leaving him—and in any case they had not the value of those won from bragging opponents kneeling around a circle drawn in the earth.

'Is the chair high enough, would you like a cushion? . . . You must work hard if you want to get near the top of your class, but you must *enjoy* working...There! Now I'll do my sewing and not say a word.'

Hers was not big industrious sewing, complete with bee-humming machine, as at home. She sat delicately edging a tiny handkerchief with a shred of lace, and on her face was a look of minutes strained to their utmost; she had the manner of one who never glances at a clock. The house was tidy, clean, respectably comfortable. But it was shabbier than his own home. And somehow without atmosphere, as if it was left alone to look after itself and no love or hate clashed within its shiny darkly-papered walls. Occasionally this lack of something important vaguely bothered the boy. He would stand with his lip lifted, his nostrils dilated. He had never been upstairs, and he always wanted to penetrate its privacy. Was the thing he missed to be found there? Did they live up there and only come downstairs when there were visitors? Down here it was all parlour and Sunday silence, with for movement only the lonely goldfish eternally circling its bowl.

Mr. Mitchell came in before the homework was finished. 'Good evening, *sir*,' he greeted Nicholas. 'Doing my accounts for me?' He seemed to look at the boy and yet not look at him. And he was not a jocular man. He had a full, dahlia-red, rather staring face of flabby contours, sagged in on its own solitude and the eyes did not seem to connect with the object they looked at. His face had affinities with the face of some floridly ponderous beast. He had a very thick neck. It was strange, and yet not at all strange, that his work had to do with cattle.

'Do you want a meal now,' Mrs. Mitchell asked in the heavy silence, 'or can you wait?' Her voice was crisper; she stitched in calm withdrawal; she might have been an indifferent daughter. Though bent at the table, the boy sensed the change. There was a cold air of armistice in the room, of emptiness. Nervously he opened his bottle of lemonade. The explosion of the uncorking sounded very loud.

'I'll go upstairs,' Mr. Mitchell said. 'Yes, I'll go upstairs. Call me down.'

'You'll hear the dishes,' she said concisely. The boy turned and saw her stitching away, like a queen in a book of tales. Mr. Mitchell went out bulkily; his head lolled on the fleshy neck. It was as if he said 'Pah!' in a heavily angry way. His footsteps were ponderous on the staircase.

Had he come straight from the slaughter-house and was weary? Had he a short time ago been killing cattle? Nicholas, like all the boys of the place, was interested in the slaughter-house, a squat building with pens and sties in a field down by the river. Once he had been allowed inside by an amiable young assistant who understood his curiosity, and he saw in a white-washed room hung with ropes and pulleys a freshly dead bullock strung up in the air by its legs; it swayed a little and looked startlingly foolish. Blood spattered the guttered floor and some still dripped from the bullock's mouth like a red icicle. In a yard another young man was rinsing offal in a tub filled with green slime. 'No, we're not killing pigs today,' he replied to Nicholas's enquiry. Because of the intelligent squeals and demented hysteria of these intuitive beasts as they were chased from the sties into the house of death, pig-killing was the prized spectacle among all the boys. But few had been fortunate enough to witness it; the slaughter-men usually drove them away from the fascinating precincts. Nicholas, an unassertive boy on the whole, had never liked to take advantage of his friendship with the Mitchells and ask to be taken to the place properly, an accredited visitor on a big day. He wondered if Mrs. Mitchell went there herself sometimes. Could she get him a pig's bladder?

She did not bring in supper until he had finished the homework. 'There, haven't I been quiet?' she smiled. 'Did you work easily? I can see you're studious and like quiet. Do you like lobster too?'

'Lobster?' He looked at her vacantly.

She fetched from the kitchen an oval dish in which lay a fabulous scarlet beast. Cruel claws and quiveringly-fine feelers sprang from it. At first he thought that Mr. Mitchell must have brought it from the slaughter-house, but when his excitement abated he remembered they came from the sea. 'How did you get it?' he asked, astonished.

'I have to ask Harris's fish shop to order one especially for me. I'm the only person here that wants them.'

'Do they cost a lot?'

Over the fiery beast she looked at him conspiratorially.

'Nothing you enjoy ever costs a lot,' she smiled mysteriously.

Mr. Mitchell must have heard the dishes, but he came down looking more torpid than ever. 'Lobster again!' he said, sombrely. 'At night? There's stomachs of cast-iron in this world.'

Mrs. Mitchell looked at him frigidly. 'If you encourage nightmares they'll come,' she said.

'You're not giving it to the boy?' he said.

'Why not? You'll have a little, Nicholas?' Of course he would.

'I have dreams,' said Mr. Mitchell, his heavy dark-red face expressionless. 'Yes, *I* have dreams.'

'Do you?' Her husband might have been an acquaintance who had called at an inopportune time. 'A little salad, Nicholas? Shall I choose it for you?' In delightful performance she selected what seemed the best pieces in the bowl; with deft suggestions she showed him how to eat the lobster. He enjoyed extracting from inside a crimson scimitar shreds of rosily white meat. The evening became remarkable for him.

And it was because of it he added to the local legend of Mrs. Mitchell. When he told them at home about the lobster there was at first a silence. His mother glanced up, his brothers and sisters were impressed. He felt superior. A couple of weeks later, while he waited to be served in Watkins's shop just after Mrs. Mitchell had passed the window on her return from her walk, he heard a collier's wife say: 'Yes, and they say she has lobsters for breakfast nearly every day. No doubt her new hat she wears at breakfast too, to match them.' Despite his sense of guilt, he felt himself apart, an experienced being. No one else in the place was known to have dealings with the exotic fish.

'She'll be giving him champagne next,' he heard his father say to his mother. 'Mitchell, poor devil, will be properly in the soup some day.' And his mother said, troubled. 'Yes, I *do* wonder if Nick ought to go there—'

III

That winter Mrs. Mitchell won a £100 prize in a periodical which ran a competition every week. You had to make up a smart remark on a given phrase and send it in with a sixpenny postal order. A lot of people in the place did it; someone else had won £10, which set more members of both sexes running to the Post Office. It seemed quite in order that Mrs. Mitchell, who dressed like no one else, should win a cracker of a prize, but everybody was agog the day the news got around.

'You'll be going to see her every day now,' Nicholas's eldest brother jeered, adding offensively: 'Take your money-box with you.' And his father said to his mother, in that secret-knowledge way which roused an extra ear inside one: 'If she's got any feeling, she'll hand it to Mitchell straight away.' To this his mother said: 'Not she!'

A week later, with Christmas not far off, Mrs. Mitchell took her afternoon walk in a new fur coat. It shone with an opulent gleam as if still alive and its owner walked with the composure of one who owns three hundred and sixty-five fur coats. It was treated to a companionable new hat into which a blue quill was stabbed cockily as a declaration of independence. Her red tasselled umbrella, exquisitely rolled, went before her with a hand attached lightly as a flower. The women watchers down the long bleak road gathered and stared with something like consternation. Surely such luxury couldn't proceed for ever! The God of Prudence, who had made his character known in abundant scriptures, must surely hurl one of his thunderbolts right in her path some day.

That same evening Nicholas visited the Mitchells' house. And he found Mrs. Mitchell delicately shedding a few tears into a lacy wisp of the finest linen. He could not take this restrained sort of weeping seriously. Especially as she had just won a big prize. 'Have you got a headache?' he asked.

She blew her pretty nose and dried her tears. 'I'm glad you've come. It keeps Mr. Mitchell quiet.' Pointing to the ceiling, she whispered dramatically: 'He's just gone up . . . Oh dear!' she sighed.

'What is he always doing upstairs?' It did not now take him long to adjust himself to being treated as a grown-up.

'Oh, only sleeping . . . He's a man that seems to need a great deal of sleep. He says he gets bad dreams, but I believe he likes them.' She smiled at him with dainty malice. 'Do you know what he wanted? . . . My prize!' Nicholas looked thoughtful, like one privy to other knowledge. She went on: 'Week after week I worked so hard at those competitions, and he never helped me, it was all my own brains.' Her eyes shone with that refined malice. 'To tell you the truth, *he isn't clever*. Not like you and me.' She giggled. 'Oh dear, don't look so solemn, Nicholas; I've had a very trying day.'

'I have too,' he said.

'Have you, darling? Would you like a chocolate?' She jumped up and fetched a large ribboned box from the sideboard. They ate in release from the stress. But he could see her attention was on something else, and presently resumed: 'He found out today that I spent the prize on a fur coat. Oh good gracious, such a fuss!' She rummaged for other chocolates. 'An almond one this time? Nougat? I don't like the peppermint ones, do you? We'll keep them for Mr. Mitchell . . . Of course, people do criticise me,' she said, wrinkling her nose. 'You must not repeat what I've said, Nicholas.'

'Oh no,' he said, decided but flushing. Memory of the lobster affair still obscurely troubled him.

'Gentlemen do not,' she said. 'As you know.'

'I'm going to visit my grandmother after Christmas,' he said awkwardly.

Suddenly footsteps sounded on the stairs, descending with pronounced deliberation. And Mrs. Mitchell seemed to draw herself in, like a slow graceful snail into its shell. The door opened, and Mr. Mitchell stood there in a bowler hat and overcoat, bulky and glowering. Even his ragged moustache looked as if it was alive with helpless anger—anger that would never really shoot out or even bristle. 'Am going out,' he said, in a low defeated growl. Of Nicholas he took no notice. 'Going out,' he repeated. 'Yes.'

'You are going out,' she murmured, remote in her shell. Her eyelids were down as if against some rude spectacle.

'Yes.' Something in his heavy neck throbbed, making it thicker. Yet there was nothing threatening in his mien. His slow, ox-coloured eyes travelled from his wife's face to the large pink box of chocolates on her knees. 'I hope,' he then said, 'you'll always be able to afford 'um.'

She asked faintly: 'What time will you be back? Supper will—'

'Going to the slaughter-house,' he said sullenly. 'Got a job to do.'

'—-will be ready at nine,' she said.

'Ha!' he said. He stared at her shut face. But the heavy gaze of his unlit eyes threw out no communication. The boy looked round. Feeling at a loss, he glanced uneasily at Mrs. Mitchell and saw that a peculiar, almost dirty grey, tint blotched her face. 'Ha!' repeated Mr. Mitchell. The large, sagged face hung down over his swollen neck. For a moment he looked vaguely menacing. Then he tramped into the hallway. The front door slammed.

Mrs. Mitchell opened her eyes wide at the slam. 'Oh dear!' she wailed faintly. Her eyes were different, darker, almost black. 'He never says very much,' she fluttered, 'but he stands there *looking* . . . Good gracious!' She bit a chocolate mechanically and winced in chagrin as if it held a flavour she did not like. 'It seems he's having a very busy time in the slaughter-house,' she went on erratically; 'Some sheep have come in . . . Ah, well!' She jumped up again. 'You haven't seen my new photographs.'

Once again they sat over the album: she inserted a copy of the new photograph. There she was in about thirty different representations, but whether she was sad or smiling, dreamy or vivacious, aloof or inviting, it was clear that the eye of Mr. Burgess's camera found itself in concord with its elegant object. For nearly an hour she pored over the album with an exaggerated, detailed interest, demanding once more his opinion. Her voice was high, her manner hurried: 'Isn't this your favourite? Yes. It's mine too. Why do you like it so much?'

He thought carefully. 'You look as though you're just going for a holiday to the seaside,' he said finally.

'It's true I was happy that day. At the time I thought we were going to move to London . . . Then Mr. Mitchell refused to take the job he was offered there.' Her voice sharpened remarkably. 'He refused . . . The fact is, he has no ambition.' Suddenly she snapped the album shut, rose with a bright restlessness. 'Will you come down to the slaughter-house with me, Nicholas?'

At last the invitation! He agreed with alacrity and thought of the envy of the other boys.

'If you are with me, Mr. Mitchell won't be so disagreeable.' She hurried upstairs and returned in her new fur coat and the coquettish toque. 'Come, I didn't realise we had sat here so long . . . I can't have him sulking and going without his supper,' she explained.

The starlit night was cold. There were few people in the streets. The secret mountains smelled grittily of winter. Somewhere a dog barked insistent, shut out from a house. The public-house windows were clouded with yellow steam, and in a main-street house a woman pulled down a blind on a lamplit front parlour where sat Mr. Hopkins the insurance agent beside a potted fern. They crossed the main street and took a sloping road trailing away into waste land. Odorous of violets and dark fur, Mrs. Mitchell walked with a surprisingly quick glide; Nicholas was obliged to trot. They heard the icy cry of the river below, flinging itself unevenly among its stone-ragged banks. She said nothing now.

The slaughter-house stood back in its field, an angular array of black shadows; no light showed there. Mrs. Mitchell fumbled at the fence gate of the field. 'I've only been here once,' she said, 'when I brought down the telegraph saying his father had died.' She paused doubtfully. 'There's no light.' But the gate was unlocked.

'There are windows at the back,' Nicholas urged; 'there's a little office at the side.' But he himself was disappointed. It seemed unlikely that slaughtering was proceeding among those silent shadows.

They walked up the cobbled path. There was a double door leading into a stone-floored paddock; it swung loose. Inside, a huge sliding door led into the main slaughter-chamber; this did not yield to their push. Then Nicholas remembered the smaller door at the side; he turned its knob, and they walked into a whitewashed passage lit at the end by a naked blue gas-jet. 'The office is down there,' he said. He felt morose and not implicated; he remembered glancing into the office during his previous visit; it was no more than a large box with a table and chair and files and ledgers. They walked down the stone-flagged passage. She stopped. He heard her breathing.

'Go back,' she said.

Sharpened by her tone of command, he looked up at her. Her nostrils, blue in the gaslight, were quivering. He looked down quickly. From under a door a stream of dark thick liquid had crawled. It was congealing on the stone flag into the shape of a large root or a strand of seaweed. He looked at it, only distantly conscious of her further cry and her fingers pressing into his shoulders. 'Go back; go home,' she exclaimed. He did not move.

She stepped to the door as if oblivious of him. But she carefully avoided the liquid root. She turned the brass knob, slowly pushed back the door. Still the boy had not moved. He could not see inside the door. She gave a queer cry, not loud, a low hunted cry broken in her mouth. And Nicholas never forget the gesture with which her hand went to her throat. He ran forward from the wall. At the same time his feet instinctively avoided the dark smears. 'Let me see!' he cried. But she pulled back the door. 'Let me see!' he cried. It was then he became conscious of another odour, a whiff from the closing door mingled with the perfume of fur and violets.

She violently pushed him back. 'Go home at once!' There was something like a terrible hiss in her voice. He looked up in confusion. Her face, blotched with a sickly pallor, was not the elegantly calm face he knew; the joints and muscles had loosened and were jerking convulsively. It was as if the static photograph of a pleasing face had in some nightmare way suddenly broken into ugly grimaces. For a moment he stared aghast at that face. Then he backed from her.

Her eyes seemed not to see him. 'Go!' she screamed, even

more startlingly. Then he swiftly turned and ran.

IV

Three days later, carrying a large bunch of chrysanthemums from his mother, he walked down to the Mitchells' house. He went with a meek unwillingness. But not unconscious of the drama in which he was involved. All those three days the place had hummed with talk of the Mitchells'. Within living memory there had been only one local suicide before.

Already there was pre-knowledge of the bailiffs who were only waiting for the coffin to leave the house before taking possession. The dead man's affairs were in shocking condition. Besides forcing him to mortgage his house several years ago, the Fashion Plate had bullied him into going to moneylenders . . . And no, she was not a nagging woman, but she got her way by slyly making him feel inferior to her. She had done him honour by marrying him and he must pay for what was necessary to her selfish happiness.

At first Nicholas's mother had said he must not visit the house again. Then that evening— the inquest had taken place the previous day—she told him to take the flowers. His unwillingness surprised her and, oddly enough, made her more decided that he should go on this compassionate errand. He frowned at the flowers but sheltered them from the wind. He wondered if it was true that the Mitchells' house was going to be sold up, and if so could he ask for the goldfish.

When Mrs. Mitchell opened the door he looked at her

with a furtive nervousness. But, except for the deep black of her shinily flowing new frock, she was no different. 'Oh, Nicholas darling!' she greeted him, with the same composed smile as before the event. And she accepted the flowers as if they were for an afternoon-tea vase. She was alone in the house. But twice there was a caller who was taken privately into the front room for a short while.

'You haven't brought your homework with you?' she asked. He was a little shocked. Upstairs lay the dead man in his coffin. She sat making calculations and notes in a little book. A heap of black-edged stationery lay on the table. The pit hooter sounded. There were silences. He looked at the goldfish eternally circling its bowl— 'What do you feed it with?' he murmured at length.

'Black gloves—' she said inattentively, 'do you think I could find a decent pair in this hole of a place!'

Out of the corner of his eye he kept on glancing at her, furtively. Once she remarked: 'You are very distant this evening, Nicholas.' Then, as his silences did not abate, she asked suddenly: 'Well, haven't you forgiven me?' He looked confused, and she added: 'For pushing you away so rudely in the slaughter-house.' The cloudy aloofness in his mind crystallised then, and he knew he indeed bore her a grudge. She had deprived him of something of high visual interest. In addition he was not yet reconciled to the revelation of how she had *looked* . . . 'Oh, it doesn't matter,' he mumbled, with hypocritical carelessness. He stared again at the goldfish. 'What do you feed the goldfish with?' he repeated.

'You must take that goldfish away with you tonight. Otherwise those dreadful men will stick a number on the bowl and get half a crown for it . . . Would you like to see Mr. Mitchell now?' As he did not reply at once but still looked owlish, she said: 'Well, come along upstairs.' He rose and followed her, in half forgiveness. 'I don't like being depressed, it doesn't suit me,' she complained, 'I feel quite old.'

Her fresh poplin skirts hissed as she climbed. 'Poor Mr. Mitchell,' she sighed, 'I do wish I could feel more sorry for him. But I'm afraid his nature made him melancholy, though I must say as a young man he wasn't so difficult . . . And he used to be quite handsome, in a footballer kind of way . . . Ah!' she said, shaking her head, 'these beefy sportsman types, they're often quite neurotic, just bundles of nerves . . . Oh, it's all been so unpleasant,' she went on, with a dainty squirm of repudiation, 'but I must own he had the decency to do it *down there*.'

Upstairs there were the same four rooms as in his own home. She took him into the end back room and turned on the light. It seemed to be the room where they had slept, there were brushes on the dressing-table and a man's jacket was still flung across a chair. On the bed lay a coffin. It sank heavily into the mattress. The lid lay against a wall. 'You won't want to be here long,' she suggested, and left him to his curiosity. He saw her go across the landing to the main front room and put on the light there. She left both doors open.

He looked into the coffin. Mr. Mitchell wore a crisp white shroud which somehow robbed him of the full powerfulness of being a man. And his face, with the dark red flabbiness drained out of it, was not his. He looked as if he had been ill in bed for a long time but was now secure in a cold sort of health. Round his throat a folded white napkin was tightly swathed. This linen muffler, together with the shroud, gave him an air of being at the mercy of apparel he would not himself have chosen. Nicholas' round eyes lingered on the napkin.

He left the room feeling subdued and obedient. The cold isolation of the dead man lying helpless in that strange clothing made him feel without further curiosity; there was nothing to astonish, and nothing to startle one into fearful pleasure.

Mrs. Mitchell heard him come out and called: 'What do you think of this, Nicholas?' He went along the landing to the fully illuminated front room and saw at once it was where she slept. The room was perfumed and untidy with women's clothes strewn everywhere. Hadn't Mr. and Mrs. Mitchell used the same room, then, like other married people? He looked around with renewed inquisitiveness. A large cardboard hat-box lay open on the bed. From it Mrs. Mitchell was taking a spacious black hat on which the wings of a glossy blackbird were trimly spread in flight. Standing before the mirror she carefully put on the hat.

Even he could see it was an important hat. She turned and smiled with her old elegant brilliance. 'I'm wearing it to London as soon as Mr. Mitchell is buried. My sister is married to a publican there...Do you like it?' she asked in that flattering way that had always nourished him and made him feel that he was a full-size man of opinions.

A HUMAN CONDITION

Having done the errand at the Post Office, which he had timed with a beautiful precision that he imagined completely hoodwinked those left at home, Mr. Arnold crossed the Market Square just as the doors of the Spreadeagle inn were opened.

This morning he was in lamentable condition. He felt he would never get through the day without aid. Never, never, never. Deep inside him was a curious dead sensation of which he was frightened. It lay in the pit of his stomach like some coiled serpent fast asleep, and he was fearful that at any moment the thing would waken and writhe up in unholy destructive fury. And ultimately *he* would be destroyed. Not his critics, today collected in dark possession of his home.

He sailed into the pub with his ample, slightly rolling strut, a man of substance handsomely ripe of body and face, his attire as conservative as a psalm to godliness; no one could say Mr. Arnold neglected his person. Of the town's few pubs the Spreadeagle was his favourite haunt. It was cosily shut in on itself and dark with shadows; it had low, black-beamed ceilings, copper gleams, honest smells, and morose windows hostile to light. In the hall a torpid spaniel bitch looked at him with the heavily drooping eyes of a *passée* actress; she knew Mr. Arnold, and there was no necessity for even a languid wag of her tail. Always the first customer, he stepped into the bar parlour with his usual opening-time briskness. But Mrs. Watson, polishing glasses behind the bar, looked at him with a start. 'Well!' she seemed about to exclaim, but only pursed her lips.

'A whisky,' he said; 'a double.'

'A double?' Something was concealed in her tone.

'Yes, for God's sake.' The false briskness was suddenly deflated. 'And pour another for me while you're about it.'

'*No*, Mr. Arnold,' she said, flat; 'no. Not *two* doubles . . . It isn't right,' she bridled; 'not today. Good heavens! Don't forget you've got to be there sober at two o'clock. *No*, Mr. Arnold.'

'Hell!' he muttered. He looked over his shoulder with child-blue eyes round in fear. 'Where's Alec?' A man would understand, must surely understand, what that day really meant. Women were incalculable in the domain of the affections, could run so drastically from the extremes of loving solicitude to the bleakest savagery. 'Where's Alec?' he peered.

'Gone to London for the day,' his wife said. 'Gone to buy me a budgerigar.'

'Gone to London,' he mumbled, preoccupied.

'They can chirp ever so sweet,' she said tightly, 'and intelligent, my goodness! – my sister had one that would hop on the table when she was making cake and stone the raisins for her.'

'What?' He started from his glassy preoccupation.

'The budgerigar she had. With its beak. Intelligent, my stars! . . . I've known many a human being,' she said forbiddingly, 'that could do with their brains and feelings.'

Both the Malt Shovel and the Bleeding Horse, which were on his way, were only beer houses. No licence for spirits. But there was plenty of time. He would climb to Cuckoo Ridge, up to the Self Defence. Its landlord, whose wife had been in an asylum for years, would understand. There was the Unicorn too, nearer, but repellent with its horrible modern cocktail bar, its café look, and its dirty waiters.

Mrs. Watson, solicited with flattery and whining, allowed him a single whisky more. She asked him what would be said in the town if she allowed him to have all he wanted on that morning of all mornings. He left the house with dignity, part of him pre-occupied with feeling offended, but the greater part obeying a huge desolate urge to complete the scarcely begun journey into that powerful state where he would feel secure, a captain of his fate, if a melancholy one. He had never been able to take to drinking at home. Besides, Susan never encouraged it. Never a bottle of whisky in the house.

In the shopping street, those people who knew Mr. Arnold—and they were many, for by now he was a local celebrity—looked at him with their cheerfulness, due to the brilliant day, wiped momentarily from their faces. But he encouraged no one to pass a few words with him; time must not be wasted. He took a side turning and began to climb among loaded apple and pear trees spread over garden walls. The whole fragrantly warm little town was fat with sunlight, fruit and flowers. Mr. Arnold began to pant and lean on his expensive malacca stick.

Above, on the bright emerald slopes with their small well-groomed fields, cows stood like shiny china ornaments. The short local train from London puffed a plume of snowy cotton-wool. It was toy countryside, and Mr. Arnold felt obliged to admire its prettiness; it had been Susan's idea to live here on his retirement from his highly successful career in the City lanes near Tower Bridge, where scores of important men knew him. He liked to feel that London was still near, he liked to see, on Sundays and Bank Holidays, clumps of pallid cockney youths and girls in cycling knickers dotting those slopes like mushrooms. The high air, clear as mineral waters, was supposed to be good for one. Susan said it eased her chest, and she had become a leading voice in the Women's Institute . . . Ah, Susan, Susan! Her husband panted in sore distress, climbing.

On Cuckoo Ridge the landlord of the Self Defence greeted him, after a slight pause, courteously. But Mr. Arnold saw at once that he was in the know. Rapidly he asked for a second double. The landlord, a stout, placid man in braces, looked at him. Perhaps he saw a man in agony of spirit; he served the drink. Mr. Arnold thought he felt deep sympathy flowing from this man whose own wife had been shut away from him for several years already. He asked for a third double.

The landlord mournfully shook his head. 'Best not, Mr. Arnold.'

'One more,' panted Mr. Arnold. 'Only one. I've got a day in front of me.' In the pit of his stomach was a stirring of fear, as if the sleeping coil shuddered. 'Never be able to face it,' he whimpered.

The landlord shook his head in slow, heavy decision. 'There's the circumstances to consider,' he said.

Mr. Arnold attempted a hollow truculence. 'My money's as good as anyone's—'

'Now, sir,' said the landlord distantly, 'best be on your way.' And, solemnly: 'You've got a job to do, Mr. Arnold.'

Mr. Arnold walked out with deliberate steadiness. A clock had struck twelve-thirty. It would have to be the Unicorn, and time was pressing now. Actually he had already taken his morning allowance, but today . . . today... He descended from the Ridge with a careful step, crossed the watercress beds into the London road, and looked sourly at the gimcrack modern façade of the Unicorn, a rebuilt house done up for motoring whipper-snappers and their silly grinning dolls. He went in like an aggressive magistrate with power to deprive the place of its licence. But he cast himself into a bony scarlet-and-nickel chair with a groan, wiping his brow. A white presence slid up to his chair.

'Double whisky,' he said.

'Yes, Mr. Arnold,' said the waiter.

He cocked up his eye sharply. Known here too! In a blurred way, the grave young face looking down at him was familiar. Ha, it was Henry, who used to come with his father to do the garden! Quickly Mr. Arnold assumed the censorious glare of a boss of substance. 'And mind it's genuine Scotch, Henry,' he said. He did not like the boy's solicitous look as he withdrew to the blonde cinema star serving behind the jazzy zigzagged corner counter. He took out his big presentation gold watch and looked at it importantly. Was there a pausing at the bar, a whispering? Surely he, who had been a guest at Lord Mayor's banquets in the Mansion House, was not going to be dictated to in a shoddy hole like this? Henry brought the double. 'Get me another, my boy,' Mr. Arnold said. Henry hesitated, but withdrew; came back— 'Sir,' he said awkwardly, 'sir, there's no more except this single. Our supplies haven't arrived; they'll be here by tonight.' Was everybody his enemy that day? Was there a plot against him? After that long walk, to be allowed only this! Mr. Arnold pushed back his chair, made an effort to collect his forces for dire protest. But somehow—was it because of guilt or the hear?—they would not assemble. He could only gaze fixedly at Henry in silent reproach, anger, and finally, entreaty. 'Very sorry, sir,' mumbled Henry from far away. 'Can I call up the garage for a taxi, sir?'

'A taxi? Certainly not.' He swallowed the single, tipped lavishly, rose like an offended emperor, sat down, and rose again, thunderous yet dignified.

'Your stick, Mr. Arnold.' Henry handed it.

He needed it now. Outside, his eyes could focus neither on the shifting ground nor the burning pansy-coloured sky. The soft amateur hills ran into each other like blobs of water-colours imperfectly handled. But he would walk, he would walk. Anything rather than be in the house before it was quite essential. Not with *them* there . . . The town hall clock, its notes gently without chiding, struck the quarter after one. Yet those chimes were like knells bringing grief. Grief, grief. A sensation of burning grief, physical and staggering, pierced him. He sat gasping on the low roadside wall. The day was no longer brilliant, crackling with sun. The desolation of what awaited his presence swept down on him in gusts of black depression. God above, he could never face it. Not without—. He rose with remarkable celerity.

Fool, fool! Why had he forgotten the Adam and Eve? He walked rapidly, a man refreshed, stick striking the road almost evenly . . . But outside the Adam and Even, a sixteenth-century house sagging in a dark medieval alley hidden in the town, he paused to arrange himself into the aspect of a man with a grip on himself, and he rolled into the pub with a lordly assurance.

The poky, cool bar parlour was deserted except for a cat enormously asleep on the counter. Mr. Arnold called: 'Hey! Customer here!' He banged the counter with his stick. No one appeared. Not a sound shifted into the stagnant air. He gave the cat a sharp dig with his stick; it did not stir or open an eye. He shouted, thumped the counter. A dead petal of plaster fell from the ceiling. But no one came. The silence closed impervious over his shouts of anguish. No one passed in the shadowed alley outside. His stick rang frenziedly on the counter. He had the feeling he was in a dream in which a ghostly, senseless frustration dogs one's every move. The cat slept. The hands of a dusty old clock remained neatly and for ever together at twelve o'clock. The bottles on the shelves looked as if they were never opened. He jabbed the cat again; it did not move out of its primeval sleep.

Mr. Arnold whimpered. He lurched over to the door in the crooked bellied-out wall and lifted the old-fashioned latch. But the door wouldn't open. Had it been locked behind him? Was he being imprisoned? 'Who's there?' he screamed, banging his stick furiously against the rickety panel. The after-silence did not budge. He tore madly at the latch. Suddenly the door flew open; it had jammed in the ancient frame. Raging, Mr. Arnold stamped down the passage, threw back another door.

A dazzle of pink interior light struck into his eyes. He stepped into a hot living-room with a huge window and an opened door leading to a garden blazing with snapdragons, roses and hollyhocks. A blue-gowned woman, immensely fat, was pegging out washing over the gush of flowers. Mr. Arnold all but sobbed with relief. 'Customer!' he yelled.

'Be there in a minute,' she called affably. 'It's a beautiful drying day.'

'Got a train to catch,' he bellowed. 'I want a double Scotch.'

'All right, all right.' Smooth and brown-faced as an egg, and with a dewlap of Turkish chins, she indolently left her basket, saying: 'No need to be crotchety. Where there's one train there's another; they've got the extra summer service now to London. I'm going up myself on Thursday; my daughter's going to be examined . . . Why, it's Mr. Arnold!' She paused, in pastoral caution. 'Are they taking her by train, then? I didn't know.' As if this settled her doubt, she hurried into the bar.

Mr. Arnold said nothing. He drank the double in two gulps and asked for another, saying quickly: 'Then I've got to hurry.' The woman talked of her daughter with soft, unstressed tact. He paused uncertainly after the second double.

'No, Mr. Arnold,' she decided for him, 'I can't give you any more.'

'Mrs. Busby,' he said grandly, grasping his stick as for a march, 'I know when to stop.'

'Gents always do,' she nodded approval. 'God bless you.'

Now he felt translated into the desired sphere, where he could survey his kingdom without lamentations. Power radiated in him. As in the old days of his office fame, he could have settled a ledger page of complicated figures in a twinkling. And that menacing dead weight in the pit of his stomach had vanished. He felt himself walking erect and proud though the luncheon-quiet town. He required no one's compassion. This heady brilliance lasted him all the way home. And he would not be late; a fixed stare at his watch testified to that. He congratulated himself on the efficient way he had handled his time. *They* would not be able to rebuke him for being late, on this day of all days.

Yet sight of his well-kept villa at the edge of the town struck a note in his soul like a buried knell. The garden, green-lawned and arched with trellises of roses, was trim beyond reproach—the packet he spent on it every year! And the house was cleanly white as a wedding cake. But quite suddenly now he felt that its walls and contents, its deeds and insurance policies, no

Rhys Davies

longer interested or concerned him. At the gate he paused in panic. Was this, the first faint rising of the horror he thought was obliterated from his being?... But almost at once this fear became blurred. His stick decisively tapping the crazy paving, he rolled up under the arches of roses with an air of having unfortunate business to transact.

The white-porched door was wide open. He entered bustlingly. Out of the drawing-room came Miriam, his elder sister-in-law; the woman in charge now, and his enemy. She looked at him and shrank. 'We waited lunch as long as we could,' she said, in her hard, gritty way. Her husband hovered behind her, thick horn glasses observant. 'I wanted George to go into the town and look for you—' she said hopelessly.

'Food!' Mr. Arnold said, in high rebuke. 'You didn't expect me to eat lunch *today*?'

They all advanced out of the drawing-room into the hall, looking at him sideways. Ellen, the younger sister-in-law, and her husband, the dentist's assistant; their grown-up daughter; and Miriam's adolescent son. Alert but careful, visitors and yet that day not visitors, they were all dressed up and important, as if they were going to be photographed. Mr. Arnold stretched his hat to a peg on the stand but miscalculated its position—'Cursed thing,' he remarked solemnly to the fallen hat. He sat heavily in the hard oak hall chair and wiped his brow. 'In good time,' he observed. 'Five minutes yet . . . What... what you all standing there for?' He jerked up his head despotically. He saw tears streaming down Ellen's face before she turned, and hurrying into the drawing-room, moaned, 'I shall be ashamed to go. He's ruined the day. Something must be done. Henry—' she motioned to her husband. But Miriam, stark and glaring, stood like judgment.

'They're coming,' called her son, who had gone to the open door and was keeping a watch on the lane.

'Two o'clock!' said Mr. Arnold in a solemn but strangely forlorn voice. 'Two o'clock!' Still collapsed in the chair, he groaned; his glassy eyes rolled, then stonily looked forth like tortoise eyes.

Henry and Ellen came back and whispered to Miriam's husband; they advanced briskly to Mr. Arnold. 'Look, old boy,' George attempted male understanding. 'We think you'd better not go with us. We will see to everything. Take it easy and have a rest.' Enticingly he laid his hand under Mr. Arnold's armpit, while Henry gripped the other arm. 'They're here; come upstairs,' he coaxed. The two sisters watched in pale, angry withdrawal.

Mr. Arnold, shaking away the possessive hands, rose from the chair tremendously. 'What!' he panted. 'Better not go!' Masterfully he drew himself up. 'Me! *Me*!'

'You are drunk,' pronounced Miriam in icy rage. 'You are blind drunk. It's shameful.' Ellen wilted with a bitter sob against the wall.

Mr. Arnold's eyes bulged. Their devilish shine enveloped Miriam with a terrible contempt, restrained for many years. 'This,' said Mr. Arnold, '*this* is no time for insults. The pack of you can clear out now if you like. *I will go alone*,' he said defiantly.

'Now look here—' George began, conciliatory but aghast.

At that moment four men loomed at the open doorway. Four tall men, sleek and black-garbed, leanly efficient of aspect. With everyone in the hall black-clothed, too, the fair summer day seemed turned to shadow. The drawing-room clock struck two dainty *pings*. At the sound the four men entered, admirably prompt. There was something purifying in their sinewy impersonality. 'Upstairs,' Mr. Arnold, steady as a stout column, told them, 'in the dark room.' The black quartet filed up the staircase. Out of the kitchen came Mrs. Wills, her apron removed, and stood apart with her kind cook's fist under an eye.

'Have you decided to risk it?' Henry muttered to the women, while Mr. Arnold reached down with glacial but careful dignity for his black hat. There was whispering, a furtive watching of him.

Down the staircase came the four men with the coffin tilted on their shoulders. The seven mourners stood back. Mr. Arnold's face was stonily set again. He followed the quartet out with a stern and stiff gait. George and Henry, watchful, went close behind him. After them, in ceremonious orderliness, the others. But the two sisters, under their fashionably crisp black hats bought especially for the journey, crept forward with heads bowed very low, asking pardon of the world for this disgrace.

Mr. Arnold negotiated half the length of the crazy paving with masterful ease. Then he began to sway. A hand grasped the trellis of an arch, and a shower of pink and white petals fell on his head and shoulders; his hat dropped out of his hand. The two men took his elbows, and now he submitted to their aid. Ellen sobbed anew; and Miriam moaned: 'We can only hope people will think it's grief.' Then she hissed frantically: 'Brush those petals off him, George; he looks as if he's getting married.'

The hearse contained its burden, the three limousines behind were elegant. 'Four wreaths,' said the supported Mr. Arnold, hanging out his head like a bull. While the impersonal mutes went back to the house, the mourners disposed themselves in the cars. Though the two sisters had planned to occupy the first car with Mr. Arnold, their husbands went in with him instead. 'There, take it easy, old boy,' said George, over-friendly now. Mr. Arnold was well off and a triumphant example of industrious rectitude in the City.

'Eh?. . . eh?' said Mr. Arnold vacantly. And, sunk between the two men into luxurious cushions, he straightway went into a doze. The car began its two-mile journey with a silent, soft glide.

'We mustn't let him go right off,' Henry worried. 'Hey! Mr. Arnold, hey!'

Mr. Arnold opened his eyes ferociously. 'The best wife a man ever had,' he groaned. 'Susan, Susan!' he called wildly. The driver turned his head for a moment. 'Ha, shameful, am I!...That woman hasn't got the intelligence of a...of a...budgerigar! And no more Christian feeling than a trout. Who'd have thought she and Susan were sisters! . . . And that other one,' he grunted, 'what's her name...Ellen, always grizzling and telling Susan she was hard up and her husband kept her short—pah! . . . A depressing lot,' summed up Mr. Arnold, staring rigidly into space. Then again he called in loud anguish: 'Susan, Susan, what will I do now?'

Beads of perspiration stood on Henry's forehead. But George remained cool; despite the abuse of his wife, he even sounded affectionate—'Never mind, old chap,' he comforted the bereaved, 'it'll be over soon. But keep awake, don't let down the whole family.'

'What family?' asked Mr. Arnold. 'Got none.' And, sunk down and torpid, he seemed a secret being gathered eternally into loneliness. The two other men glanced at each other. 'Susan,' whispered Mr. Arnold, chin on chest, 'Susan...God above!' he wailed again, 'what will I do now?' They were going through the full shopping street; people stopped to look, with arrested eyes. 'The only one of the bunch to keep her sweetness,' muttered Mr. Arnold. 'Coming here in their showy hats!' he chuckled. 'But they couldn't make a man feel proud like Susan did. That time I took her to the Mansion House banquet—' But wild grief engulfed him anew. 'Susan – Susan,' he called, 'what'll I do now?'

'Here, pull yourself together,' Henry protested sharply at last, and, perhaps feeling Mr. Arnold had gone far enough in insults, 'We're coming to the cemetery.'

Mr. Arnold heaved into physical alertness for the ordeal. In a minute or two the car slid to a delicate standstill. Inside the cemetery gates was a group of half-a-dozen women, representatives of the institute for which Susan had organised many an event. Out of the lodge came the surpliced vicar, prayer book in hand. Henry got out first and, red-faced, offered a hand to Mr. Arnold, who ignored it and alighted without mishap. But for an awful moment the widower's legs seemed boneless. Then he drew himself up nobly, stood rock-like in ruminative strength, while the coffin was drawn out and borne ahead.

The two sisters stood in helplessness, hiding their faces, but peering like rabbits. The procession began to form. The vicar turned the pages of his book in mild abstraction. George and Henry sidled up beside Mr. Arnold. 'I'll walk alone,' hissed Mr. Arnold, and he reminded them fiercely that Miriam and Ellen were entitled to follow immediately behind him. He insisted on that being arranged. The institute women, who seemed unaware of anything unusual, took their places in the rear. The cortege moved.

The cemetery was cut out of a steepish slope, and the newly acquired section was at the top. It was quite a climb for elderly mourners; a discussion had waged in the local paper about the lack of foresight in not making a carriage road through the place. Mr. Arnold, close behind the coffin and without his well-known stick, negotiated the climb with an occasional lapsing of his knees, a straightening of his back, or a rigid turning and jerking of his head, like a man doing physical exercises. But he achieved it victoriously. Behind him Ellen wept and Miriam stared in blank fear.

It was not until all were assembled before the graveside and the service had begun that Mr. Arnold began to display signs of collapse. He vaguely swayed: his head lolled. George and Henry took a step nearer him. The abstract vicar droned unseeing; the institute women remained tactful behind the chief mourners. The attendants took up the roped coffin; it disappeared; a handful of earth was thrown in after it. Presently the vicar's voice stopped. George and Henry took Mr. Arnold's elbows to assist him for the last look.

'Leave me alone,' Mr. Arnold muttered, drawing his elbows angrily away. What had these to do with him! He advanced with renewed dignity to the brink of the grave. Looked in as if into an abyss of black tremendous loneliness. Stood there staring down in concentrated intentness, prolonged, fascinated. The vicar waited in faint surprise at the mourner's lengthy scrutiny.

George and Henry darted forward. Too late. While a single hysterical woman's cry shot up, Mr. Arnold shot down, falling clumsily, arms flapping out, his disappearing face looking briefly astonished, the mouth wide open and showing all his artificial teeth. There was a moment's hesitation of unbelieving dismay. Then the bustling began. Mr. Arnold lay down there on his stomach across the coffin. An upper denture gleamed out in the clay beside him.

'I knew it,' said Miriam, later, 'I felt it in my bones when you two allowed him to walk alone to the graveside. Thank heaven we don't live here.' They were in the villa in conference. Mr. Arnold had been taken to the county hospital with a fractured leg.

He stayed there two months. The first patient to be received out of a grave, he was the talk and pet of the hospital; as the night sister remarked: 'He must have been a devoted husband to throw himself into his wife's grave like that! I've never known a man grieve so much. How he calls out in the night for his

Susan!'…Cantankerous at first, he became astonishingly meek. The doctor allowed him a certain amount of whisky. The night sister, perhaps because she was shortly due for retirement, secretly allowed him a little more. She took quite a fancy to him, and some months later, thinking he had detected in her a flavour of Susan's character, Mr. Arnold married her.

Rhys Davies

Rhys Davies *(9 November 1901 – 21 August 1978)*
BOOKS:
The Song of Songs and Other Stories (London: Archer, 1927);
Aaron (London: Archer, 1927);
The Withered Root (London: Holden, 1927; New York: Holt, 1928);
A Bed of Feathers (London: Mandrake, 1929; New York: Black Hawk, 1935);
Tale (London: Lahr, 1930?);
Rings on Her Fingers (London: Shaylor, 1930; New York: Harcourt, Brace, 1930);
The Stars, the World, and the Women (London: Jackson, 1930);
A Pig in a Poke (London: Joiner & Steele, 1931);
A Woman (London: Capell/Bronze Snail Press, 1931);
Arfon (London: Foyle, 1931);
Daisy Matthews and Three Other Tales (Waltham Saint Lawrence, U.K.: Golden Cockerel, 1932);
Count Your Blessings (London: Putnam, 1932; New York: Covici-Friede, 1932);
The Red Hills (London: Putnam, 1932; New York: Covici-Friede, 1933);
Love Provoked (London: Putnam, 1933);
One of Norah's Early Days (London: Grayson, 1935);
Honey and Bread (London; Putnam, 1935);
The Things Men Do: Short Stories (London: Heinemann, 1936);
A Time to Laugh (London: Heinemann, 1937; New York: Stackpole, 1938);
My Wales (London: Jarrolds, 1937; New York: Funk & Wagnall's, 1938);
Jubilee Blues (London & Toronto: Heinemann, 1938);
Under the Rose (London: Heinemann, 1940);
Sea Urchin: Adventures of Jorgen Jorgensen (London: Duckworth, 1940);
Tomorrow to Fresh Woods (London: Heinemann, 1941);
A Finger in Every Pie (London: Heinemann, 1942);
The Story of Wales (London: Collins, 1943; New York: Hastings House, 1943);
The Black Venus (London: Heinemann, 1944; New York: Howell Soskin, 1946);
Selected Stories (London & Dublin: Fridberg, 1945)
The Trip to London: Stories (London: Heinemann, 1946; New York: Howell Soskin, 1946);
The Dark Daughters (London: Heinemann, 1947; Garden City, N.Y.: Doubleday, 1948);
Boy with a Trumpet (London: Heinemann, 1949; Garden City, N.Y.: Doubleday, 1951);
Marianne (London: Heinemann, 1951; Garden City, N.Y.: Doubleday, 1952);
The Painted King (London: Heinemann, 1954; Garden City, N.Y.: Doubleday, 1954);
No Escape, by Davies and Archibald Batty (London: Evans Bros., 1955);
The Perishable Quality (London: Heinemann, 1957);
The Darling of Her Heart and Other Stories (London: Heinemann, 1958);
Girl Waiting in the Shade (London: Heinemann, 1960);
The Chosen One and Other Stories (London: Heinemann, 1967; New York: Dodd, Mead, 1967);
Print of a Hare's Foot (London: Heinemann, 1969; New York, Dodd, Mead, 1969);
Nobody Answered the Bell (London: Heinemann, 1971; New York: Dodd, Mead, 1971);
Honeysuckle Girl (London: Heinemann, 1975).
COLLECTIONS:
Collected Stories (London: Heinemann, 1955);
The Best of Rhys Davies (Newton Abbot, U.K. & North Pamfret, Vt.: David & Charles, 1979).
The Collected Stories of Rhys Davies (Gomer – Three Volumes. Edited by Meic Stephens 1996)

OTHER:
Anna Kavan, *Julia and the Bazooka*, edited, with an introduction, by Davies (London: Owen, 1970);
Kavan, *My Soul in China*, edited, with an introduction, by Davies (London: Owen, 1975)
Rhys Davies, Decoding the Hare, edited by Meic Stephens, (UWP, 2001)